I0744745

Ash

HEARTS AND ASHES
BOOK TWO

IRISH WINTERS

COPYRIGHT

Ash, Hearts and Ashes, Book 2

Copyright ©2018 by Irish Winters
All rights reserved

First Edition

This is a work of fiction. Names, characters, dialogues, places, and incidents either are the product of the author's imagination or are used fictitiously. Any resemblance to actual events, locales, or persons, living or dead, is entirely coincidental. The publisher does not have any control over and does not assume responsibility for author or third-party websites or their content.

No part of this book may be reproduced, scanned, or distributed in any printed or electronic form without permission. Please do not participate in or encourage piracy of copyrighted materials in violation of the author's rights. Purchase only authorized editions.

Cover design by Letitia Hasser, Romantic Book Designs, http://www.rbadesigns.com
Interior book design by Bob Houston, eBook Formatting

ISBN Paperback: 978-1-942895-83-1
ISBN eBook: 978-1-942895-62-6

Irish Winter's author websites are:
http://www.irishwinters.com and irishwinters.blogspot.com

ACKNOWLEDGEMENTS

First to my husband, Bill, who reminds me often that I'm living my dreams. Thanks for supporting me, sweetheart. You are and always will be my sexiest hero. Love you still. Always will.

To my beta readers, my reviewers, my editor, and proofreader, (you know who you are) thank you from the bottom of my heart. They say it takes a village to raise a child. Well, it takes an army of extra eyes to smooth out the rough edges of a novel. I think back to the days before typewriters and computers, and I'm amazed at the masterpieces that have been penned by hand. They are a testament to the human spirit. And to dreams...

To my fantabulous cover artist, Letitia Hasser, you rock! I've loved every minute working with you.

To a man of great patience and good humor, Robert Houston, thanks for putting up with all my last minute formatting changes. I never have to worry with you in my corner. What are we now, twenty works done, a hundred more to go? I certainly hope so.

Lastly, to my Irish mother—I know you're looking down on me, Mom. I feel those blues eyes smiling all the way from heaven. Thanks for teaching me to pray, to love, but mostly to laugh. Life is short. You showed me how to live it.

DEDICATION

Not all who wander are lost...
J. R. R. Tolkien

You can find Irish Winters on Facebook:
https://www.facebook.com/author.irishwinters

On Twitter:
https://twitter.com/irishwinters1

For news on upcoming releases, sign up
for Irish Winters' Newsletter at
IrishWinters.com/Newsletter.

For more information about all my
books, visit IrishWinters.com.

CHAPTER ONE

Nah! *It canna be!* Ash Callahan stood with his mouth agape, in shock at the wicked orange light cast off from his burning, dying woodworking shop. He might not have built it from the ground up, but watching it go up in flames hurt as much as if he had. His heart and soul and every last one of his dreams were in there, but now...

Blimey. They're gone. They're all... gone.

Grimy puddles filled with soot and cinders shimmered along the gutter and sidewalk in the morning sun. Fire hoses stretched like overfed pythons from the hydrant on the street to the rear of the warehouse. Others wound about and between the rubber boots of at least two-dozen firemen, not that they'd be working a miracle today. Like Ash, they'd arrived too late to save the pallets of expensive hardwoods he'd stored, some from far off places. India. Indonesia. Africa.

His heart stuttered in his chest. *How could this happen? To me? Now, when I'm finally turning a coin?*

Facing the gathering crowd of spectators, he felt as naked as a newborn babe. His gaze raked every last one of their faces to detect the faintest glimmer of a smile. This was no accident. He knew it to his soul. He could feel it. *Him.* Out there. Somewhere. Gloating at the evil he'd wrought. As before, getting off on another's misfortune and despair. But Jesus, Mary, and Joseph, could it really be—?

Nah. Impossible. Not after all these years. Shaking his head, Ash refused that monster's insidious toehold on his future and convinced himself this was not, could not, be—*him.*

But bullocks, the fire chief on site had already called his men to stand down. There was no need for first-responder heroics, and nothing to save. Not anymore. The fire department's continued presence was just a precaution to keep gawkers from getting too close for a selfie while Ash's future burned.

The stupid, bloody fools.

Trapped inside what was left of the groaning skeleton that had been home and family, of sorts, to the wanderer Ash had been until he'd come to America, the raging fire beast still roared to be let free. Hungry still, it seemed to want to feed on his very soul. It had nearly succeeded.

Just last night, he'd stayed 'til well past midnight in that shop, working his fingerprints smooth on his latest masterpiece. The lovely wooden chairs, rockers, and benches he crafted by hand were nothing but a means to an end. The practical side of his enterprise provided the coinage, so the dreams trapped in his heart could live and breathe and...

Gah! No more. He'd lost it all. Every chair and lathe. Every press, every mortice and tenon. Gone.

A simple Irish carpenter, he'd recently come to America. Straight from the old sod, his strong, deft fingers had been blessed with the gift of woodcarving. His latest project, a nautical figurehead of her highness, the fearsome Irish pirate queen, Grace O'Malley, had been crafted with tender loving care for some wealthy bloke up

Cape Cod way.

Only Ash had fashioned the voluptuous breasts and curvy body of that feminine work of art, the plush hips, and, yes, the beautiful face after—*her.* The woman he pined for every blessed minute of every cursed day. Most nights, too. He had a magical, almost mystical connection when it came to wood. So apparently, did the fire.

What a fool I am. Nothing to show for meself again, but for the shirt on me back.

This—this!—was supposed to have been his second chance, the one where he made good, where he built a decent business that could sustain a loving wife and family. All gone. Every last chair and customer order. Oak or cedar, pine or mahogany, it didn't matter. He lifted his fist to his teeth. *Holy Mother of God, I'm flat broke again. What'll I do now? Ye mind telling me?*

Smoke stung his eyes, searing them enough that tears fell. He took a step out of the reach of that fire beast and swiped a hand across his face, lost when he should've been found. Kicked to the curb like a lousy cur by the brutal universe when he should have been saved.

"Blimey hell," Ash growled at the smoke darkened heavens. "What's a man got to do in this world to make you happy, eh?" He would've cursed his Maker and every last one of his Catholic saints, but his mother had boxed his ears too many times in the past for him to let loose with such heinous sacrilege now. *But Mum! Me most prized pieces are in that burning rubble. Me Irish pirate queen, for the gods' sakes!*

Surely she'd understand, God bless her. Even as he allowed the thought, Ash crossed himself with a quick Father, Son, and Holy Ghost. His mother might've offered a Hail Mary if she'd been alive to see this flaming disaster, but no. Sweet Annie Callahan would never know that her youngest son had actually amounted to something other than his two favorite sins, drinking and women. She'd been gone for years, gone the way of all his lost saints. Back to heaven with all that damned smoke.

For two quid, he'd storm the barricades and challenge that fire god for admission to his building—*me feckin' building, nah yours!*—but there was no sense in it. The time for a good Donnybrook was gone, and he couldn't win a match with the Devil anyway.

Ash flexed his fingers, holding his angst at bay as the grim-eyed fire chief, Kevin Hayden, a good bloke and a solid friend, rounded the nearest thoroughly charred corner of what once was a dream come true. Waving the smoke away, he said, "A few questions if you don't mind."

Kevin hailed from the same county in Ireland as Ash. Mayo. His brogue thickened under stress, as any Irishman worth his salt should.

"Aye. As you can bloody well see, I've got nowhere to go, do I? What is it you want to know now?" Ash couldn't make his eyes move from the writhing beast that seemed to delight in destroying his future. One mighty roof joist growled back at him, then another, as they fell, tossing another raft of sparks and the blackest smoke skyward.

"You wouldn't by chance have left a can of petrol on your loading dock, would you, my boyo?"

That earned a mean stare. Was the man daft? "I keep no flammables on me property, Kev. Nah with the exotic woods I store" —bite that tongue— "stored. I'm a simple carpenter, man, nah a flamin' grease monkey."

Kevin took the hit without a blink of his gunmetal gray eyes. "Then I hate to tell you, but we're looking at arson for sure. 'Tis the Beantown Stalker, I'd bet Saint Paddy's last sixpence on it. He's torched three warehouses on the docks this month; yours makes four. We've got to be nailing his sorry arse soon."

"'Twould be good if you'd done your job a might quicker," Ash bit out. *Instead of later, though a fat lot of good it does me now.*

Instantly sorry for lashing out at his friend, Ash scratched his fingers over his shorn head, madder than hell at the utter impotence rumbling in his gut. But ye gods! Life had shit on him one too many times in his thirty-one years. By now, all his friends had wives and children, good homes, fancy houses, and better jobs. They'd amounted to something while he hadn't. Their máthairs and das were proud of them. But bad boy Ash? The know-it-all upstart who'd left his country behind?

He had nothing but a handful of sweat, cinders, and lost chances to show for his time on Earth, be it in Ireland or America. He didn't even have his mum and da nor her, the feisty woman who still had hold of his bollocks as well as the cockles of his bloody heart. This run of bad luck began the day the high-and-mighty Colby Quaid had left town to join the Army.

Damn the wee lass.

One in the chamber. Two for the show. Three to get ready and...

Time to go.

Colby Quaid stood at the front door of her buddy Smoke Montoya's hacienda, itching to leave. Her time in Sunnyvale, Texas, was done; her debt repaid. She'd already packed her gear and loaded her pistols and extra magazines. Her trusty blade, the shiny surprise she liked to save until negotiations failed, snuggled her ankle in its hidden holster. It was the one thing she never left home without.

Unbeknownst to her when she'd left Cambodia behind only a week earlier, she'd had a mission in this dusty state: Saving the former Navy SEAL, Smoke Montoya's life. He and his woman, the model Jessie West, were home from the hospital now, their harrowing adventure over. His horses grazed peaceably in the corral, while the guy who'd nearly killed Smoke and Jessie was behind bars, hopefully awaiting a death sentence for what he'd done.

For the first time in years, maybe his life, Smoke was finally in a good place. He was safe.

Colby loved this big, brash state for its standing on the death penalty alone, but it wasn't her home, nor would it be. She'd had the urge to saddle up for a couple days now, but hadn't, not until she knew for sure her buddy didn't need an Army ranger on his six any longer. Not that he ever did. Smoke was born fighting his own battles.

He didn't need anyone but Jessie West. How'd Colby know? It didn't take a genius to figure out what all that moaning and groaning coming from his bedroom this morning meant. They might've been moving furniture, but they weren't redecorating. Not by a long shot. For longer than he'd been willing to admit, Smoke's wagon had been hitched to a rising star named Jessie West.

Laying an open palm to the closed door behind her, Colby said her goodbye in the only way she knew. "Ride easy, Smoke. Sleep hard and sleep tight."

Stirring up puffs of dust with her new shitkickers, she strode to her latest bad boy, her Harley. She donned her leathers: chaps and jacket. Zipping up tight, she tucked her blonde hair under her helmet and straddled the bike. With a sigh for the friends she was leaving behind, Colby revved the hell out of her ride in a final salute to one of the few men on the planet she respected.

Smoke would go down in history for his acts of courage. Not her. She'd just done her job.

Booting the kickstand, she didn't look back as she throttled up and roared off to the West Coast. After that, Colby Quaid, one of the Army's first women Rangers and the sole heir to the mighty Quaid dynasty of Beacon Hill, planned to take the long way home.

Though California.

CHAPTER TWO

"You're telling me you have no other insurance? Nothing at all? Ye gods, man. What were you thinking?" Hammer Dugan needn't be so shocked. He'd given his best sales pitch months ago, but had Ash signed the papers committing his limited finances to yet another debt? Not bloody likely.

"So there's naught you can do for me then?" Ash had to ask. Bankruptcy seemed his only recourse, but Jesus, Mary, and Joseph. Unfilled orders—the burnt kind—meant unhappy customers, and unhappy customers meant the reputation he'd worked so hard to build these last few years was nothing but mud.

"I'm sure you signed something," Hammer mumbled over the rustle of paper shuffling. "Least, I thought you did. I was pretty hammered. Hang on a sec, mate. Lemme check."

Clank. It sounded like the phone hit his desk.

It was hard to miss the irony of their given names. Hammer being the one who got *hammered.* Ash being the loser whose life was now turned to *ashes.*

Aye, nah funny, God.

Squeezing his forehead, Ash rubbed at the migraine now firmly entrenched behind his eyeballs, battering him from inside his skull. It'd be good if Hammer found something in the pile of papers always on his desk, but chances were slim. They'd been throwing back a couple Guinnesses over that come-on-down insurance spiel, but signing on the dotted line? Ash would've remembered doing that. God almighty, if he hadn't so much bad luck, he'd have none at all.

It was a risk he'd taken with deliberate forethought, though, never expecting he'd need to replace his whole bloody inventory, not to mention the building he'd all but sold his soul for, within the month. As if there was any way that he could. His credit had burned with the fire, along with his reputation .as one of the country's premier woodcarvers. As an artist? Nothing but—ash.

Ash hated his given name as much as the POS serial arsonist stalking the docks. Why hadn't his mother named him respectable Irish names like Patrick or Sean? For the love of Mike, what madness drove a man to burn other people's property?

Again Ash considered he might have been followed to America. That this was not merely the act of the serial arsonist terrorizing Boston. That this was the calculated strike by another madman who also played with fire. But would he burn other businesses to the ground just to get back at Ash?

The phone clanked again in Ash's ear as Hammer called out something unintelligible to his secretary. Dread climbed up his neck. Not good.

He had a place in Southie, a walk-up flat fit for a single guy, but most of the time, he ended the day sleeping in the backroom at Callahan Woodworks. Some might say he was one lucky bloke not to have been there when the fire broke out. But now, he almost wished he had. He was as good as dead without his business.

Without her.

"Ash?" Hammer called out.

"Here." *Give me the bad news. I'm royally fecked. Just say it.*

A blown-out sigh and, "You're uninsured, not a good business strategy, my friend."

No shit. "Thanks anyway." Ash dropped the call, needing a Guinness, not advice. *Might as well start drowning me sorrows now.*

"You looking to lose that foot?" Colby asked point blank.

She'd stopped to refuel outside Sacramento. She'd seen the redwoods. They were—tall—and now far behind her. This side of the Pacific was as wild as the Chinese side, but more beautiful since it was American. A home on the beach in California would definitely curl her toes. But the big-bellied bruiser with his dirty motorcycle boot on her bike's high temp, shotgun tailpipe was pissing her off.

Turning his red-whiskered face, he spat to the pavement like the gentleman he was not. *Civilians.* Jerks like this guy were quick to claim the camo, and they talked as if they'd done time in the Corps like their tats and OTC medals—as in over the counter—declared, but they don't know squat. No one knew what real, up-in-your-grill combat was unless they'd been there. This guy hadn't. He was a poser. A bona fide loser. All talk, no brains, no action.

She'd take odds he hadn't earned a single one of those phony scout sniper badges pinned over the brim of his grimy baseball cap. Maybe someone ought to tell the real leathernecks about this pretender. Let them educate his dumb ass.

"I reckon you and me need to get to know each other better, little darlin'," he drawled, like that southern twang was supposed get her all hot and bothered.

Colby cocked her head, her sunglasses offering a firm wall of anonymity, and her personal favorite, her Smith and Wesson 22 Victory, already lose in her underarm holster with one in the chamber. "You reckon, huh?"

Beer Gut flashed an array of dingy yellow teeth. *Gah.* She turned her head, not surprised at his lack of dental hygiene. The scary thing was that guys like him made little children like him. Not with her, though.

He closed in for the kill. "Maybe a lot better, know what I mean, sugar?"

Stop with the smarmy name calling already.

Topping off the Harley's tank, she slapped the gas nozzle back in its slot, needing to make another couple hundred miles before she called it a day. Until this confrontation, she'd planned to make Reno by dinnertime, not to grab ass in Truckee. If Beer Gut backed off, she could still make Reno. If he didn't...

"Not interested." She stuck as close to diplomacy as she could.

Beer Gut slapped his thigh, like he was coaxing a dog to come play. "I sure wish you'd reconsider."

Good luck with that.

Looking over his shoulder, he bobbed his shaved head back at his boys, three uglier-than-shit bikers standing in the shade outside the gas station's Travel Mart, all of them watching like they had a chance in hell of bedding her.

Many have tried, boys. None had what it takes, none except... Her heart skipped a beat, damn it. *None except—no one.*

"I said no, now back off." Loud and proud, she made her point clear.

When Beer Gut scraped his boot off her tailpipe, his pudgy nose twitched. "Now look, princess, I know your type. You're on the road and you're alone. You think you're tough riding a hog all by your lonesome, but you're not. You're just a little, lost girl. What's more, I don't see nobody 'round here willing to stick his neck out for you, do you? Don't make a scene. We're just gonna talk for a spell."

And then what? Gang rape? Yeah, no.

Cocking her chin to the left, Colby pushed her Ray-Bans up into her hair and out of her way. Maybe this jerk-off needed to see the whites of her pretty gold eyes before he got the drift. "You use that line all the time?" she asked, her right hand reaching under her leather jacket, seemingly for her left breast.

His beady eyes followed her move. Like a pig in rut, the slimy tip of his tongue slid over his bottom lip. "Most girls don't need a line to do what I like 'em to," he hissed. Confident now, his chin pitched forward as if challenging her to put on a show for him.

The bloody fool. Damn. Where'd that come from? *Now I'm channeling Ash Callahan? Not hardly.*

Shifting her feet in case she had to strike first, Colby angled her shoulders to block the view of this little showdown from the nice folks inside

Travel Mart. They didn't need to see the gunplay this confrontation might end with.

As easy as pie, she eased that handy little pistol out of its snug holster and leveled it at Beer Gut's crotch. "I've got a better idea," she purred. "Why don't you go home to Mama and explain why Daddy can't play with his hairy balls anymore?"

Beer Gut lost that lusty gleam in his eye. Both meaty hands lifted palms forward, willing to placate instead of bully a lone woman traveler on the road. "I don't want no trouble."

She let her Mean Bitch loose, the one who'd earned every stripe of her sergeant's rank, three up, two down. "Then fuck off, Bozo. I've got business in Reno, and you're making me late."

When his gaze shifted over her shoulder, she knew she had trouble on her six. No matter. Four-to-one was still good odds in her line of work. "Tell your boys to back off or so help me, I'll neuter you and feed them your testicles."

He nodded even as he said, "Ah, yeah, Go 'way, Jenner. This one ain't worth tanglin' with."

Wise-guy Jenner must've thought he knew better. The asshat had the nerve to throw a leg over her bike's saddle like he owned the place.

So that's the way it's going to be.

With her pistol pointed at Beer Gut's zipper, she swiveled her head like an owl to assess the situation now gathered around her. Tall, dark, and ugly, the guy on her bike crossed his arms over his barrel chest. The German-style, spiked metal helmet with swastika decals on both sides perched on his fat head screamed white supremacist. But all she saw was another wanna-be. Another loser about to eat asphalt.

"Get off my ride," she said evenly, her heart not even close to racing. *Or I'll make you.*

They thought they were making trouble? Try storming an Al Qaeda bunker in the middle of the night, only to find an ambush, three-to-one-odds, waiting for you. Jimmy up a tourniquet with your holster because you've already used the two tourniquets and the belt you brought along for the ride. Take on a shooter from a half-mile away while lying on your belly inside an AGM-114, laser-guided Hellfire's frag zone. Yeah, these guys had no idea how to spell trouble.

He grunted, his big chest heaving under his dirty shirt. "Whatcha gonna do about it, little girl? Slap me silly?"

The two toughs standing behind him with their swaggers on, guffawed at Jenner's effeminate twist to the last words out of his mouth, which—if she had her way—would be his last. But killing him would be breaking the law, so...

With one eye still on Beer Gut, she let her fingers glide down her leg to her last chance at negotiation. If these guys were smart, they'd know what she was going for, but smart men didn't travel in packs.

Straightening, the blade now hidden up her sleeve, its grip in her palm, Colby rolled one shoulder, because, really? These guys thought they stood a chance against one of America's women Rangers? The gals who'd had to run faster and try harder to make the grade in a world of real men?

She reached up as if to run her fingers through her hair but used the momentum of that ruse to cock her arm over her shoulder. Child's play. With precise accuracy and a mental *'Up yours'* for all the defenseless women in the world, she brought the blade down and stabbed Tall, Dark, and Ugly three inches above his right kneecap.

Jenner jerked, finally getting the point. What guy wouldn't? He'd probably thought she was aiming for his balls. Expletives dribbled off his tongue, but he scrambled his ass off her bike in one helluva hurry. The two at his rear moved too. Backward.

Colby hitched her neck, just once, annoyed these guys pushed her as far as they did. "You just spoiled my day, gentlemen. Now git."

"Yes, ma'am," Beer Gut muttered, his gaze sweeping the busy gas station, no doubt scanning for witnesses or any sheriff deputy that might have been refueling.

"What? Just leave? Didn't you see what she just did? The bitch stabbed me!" Tall, Dark, and Ugly limped away with one hand on his knee.

Beer Gut kept walking, not looking back. "Told ya let her be."

"But that ain't right," TD&U sniveled. "I oughta call the cops on her."

"Do it," Colby dared them. She wouldn't put it past a gang of losers like these guys to run crying to the law when they lost the game they'd started.

"Just go," Beer Gut ordered, his fist on TD&U's elbow. "Before someone calls the cops on us."

Enough said.

Colby holstered her pride and joy after wiping her blade on one of those blue towels, the kind most folks used on their windshields. She cleaned her leather seat with another, disgusted how this chance encounter had played out.

She'd met plenty of heroes in her line of work,

and a few cowards, but the majority of soldiers were just nice guys with a need to stand up for their country, while others only stood for themselves. It was the heroes who'd always caught her eye, the stronger than most who laid down their lives for their fellow soldiers when others ran. Who stood for the weak despite the odds. Those were her type, if she had a type. Strong men with rock solid wills and stronger ethics.

In the long run, she had yet to meet that certain someone, not that she'd been looking. Her initial observation of the opposite sex still held. Men will be men. And a female Ranger will kick their asses every time.

CHAPTER THREE

Salt Lake City was nice, but Cheyenne? *My kind of town.* Rowdy. A little bit wild and rough around the edges. Colby could see herself settling down on the outskirts, maybe buying a ranch and a couple horses. Starting over. Like Smoke.

On a long stretch of never-ending highway, she cruised through Nebraska, in love with those Huskers. Her trusty bike picked up an odd vibration between Iowa City and Des Moines. Ended up being a cracked motor mount. After three hours and too many cups of bad coffee at the local Harley dealership, the problem was fixed, and her baby was as good as new.

Back on the road, Colby pointed that bad boy east and ended the day in Council Bluffs with an outrageously beautiful sunset behind her. The long way home had been a good idea. It relaxed her in ways she hadn't known she'd needed. The Harley folks were right. The sound of the road and the wind in her hair worked out the knots left by the war. Most of them anyway.

If PTSD rode with her, she didn't admit to it. Wasn't any sense in encouraging depression for things she couldn't change and wouldn't if she could. Civilians would never understand, but, as hard as combat had been, she wouldn't trade one second of her time in the Army for anything less. There was nothing better than the camaraderie of her fellow soldiers. As one of the first female Rangers, she'd had her work cut out for her, but she'd done good.

Had she called her mother with the news of that historic achievement? No reason to. Hadn't even considered it, not for a second. Bella Quaid wanted a proper daughter to climb the social ladder with her, not some tomboy who lived for soccer and came home too many nights after practice with blackened eyes or bruised ribs.

Hard work and harder play had always kept Colby's demons, if she had any, at bay. But touring the country she'd fought for and loved with all her heart? Damned good therapy, the kind she meant to repeat the first moment she could. She hadn't seen a state yet that she hadn't fallen in love with since she'd left Texas in her rearview. But that could change. Massachusetts still beckoned like a sea hag with a dirty finger, calling her back to the drama she'd left behind.

There were two reasons it was time to head home. Number one, Mom was sick. Her personal assistant, Tula, had hinted at Alzheimer's in her last lengthy text. Since Colby's father, Burton Quaid, passed when she was sixteen, there was no one else to take care of the Quaid *stuff,* for lack of a better word, which might have been *shit.*

Colby didn't want to think of the board meetings she'd have to attend as the only living heir to billions of dollars' worth of assets, some as far off as Kuala Lumpur to her west, Dubai, UAE, far to the east. Yeah. Not how she saw the rest of her life going. The mere thought of sitting in a room full of corporate types sucked the fun out of her.

Bella, Bella, Bella. Colby could almost hear the

Marlon Brando style angst in those words. Poor Bella Quaid. Life had certainly short-changed her version of the *Streetcar Named Desire*. No husband. No daughter willing to assume the burden of the family mantle, either. Yeah, it had been a tough life for one of Boston's elite widows.

Wealth and the responsibility that went with it, was nothing but a crushing load of shit Colby didn't want. *Mental note to self: Don't do this to my kids—if I ever have any. Keep 'em broke. Let 'em learn to work for a living. Teach 'em young what's important in life. Like self-worth. Pride in your country. Honesty and integrity. Those kinds of things. Money doesn't matter. Heart does.*

Number two reason? Ash Callahan. She owed the jerk. Big time. For that damned last kiss.

Next morning, she gassed up the Harley, then breakfasted at the local IHOP. You wouldn't think sitting on a bike all day worked up much of an appetite, but it did. Colby feasted on crispy bacon and eggs-over-medium with a side of blueberry pancakes. A good cup of coffee with plenty of creamer finished her off.

She hit the road again and more miles flew by. The closer she drew to Boston, Mass, the larger the knot in her gut. If things were as bad as Tula had implied...

Don't worry 'bout it. Not until you have to.

Shrugging off the negative energy worry brought with it, she cranked her speed to an even eighty miles per and hunkered into the wind. Colby let her bad boy fly.

Chapter Four

"Fecked. I'm nah only royally fecked, but I did it to meself. Bloody hell, I might as well have shot me head off. That'd solve all me troubles, eh." Ash stood with his elbows on the guard rail overlooking Boston Harbor, facing the midnight horizon to the east. Ireland lay beyond the pond, and tonight he wished he'd stayed there. That he hadn't put all his eggs in one basket. Most of all—that he'd bought an ounce of Hammer's insurance.

Nothing hurt his pride worse than admitting he'd made a mistake the size of the Emerald Isle he longed for, but he had. Aye, by hell, he had. He was what his da, if he were still alive, would call an *eejit*. Translation: *idiot.* Wasn't that the awful truth?

Stifling his regrets, Ash felt the plumbed depths of that bitter word all the way to the dregs of his soul. Like before, he had only himself to blame. Well, except for the arsonist who'd torched his building, the bastard still running fast and loose in Boston, Mass. Beantown Stalker, huh? *Wait til I get me bloody hands on 'im!*

Still, it was Ash's fault for not hedging his bets with a sound fire insurance policy. With any insurance. The bank had called before closing time—theirs, not his—inquiring after his plan for a *'sound financial remedy'*. What could he tell them, that his money tree would be bearing a bountiful harvest of quid in a day or two, so stop yer worrying? That all was well and fine in Callahan-town, when the whole city knew it wasn't?

He bowed his face to the murky waters below and pitched another cigarette butt into the swirling eddies in the harbor. *Shite, the whole world knows...*

Jesus, Joseph, and Mary, he couldn't pull one coin out of his arse, much less come up with enough green to repay the bank, replenish his inventory, and start anew. Like it or not, 'twas time to face the music. He had no plan B. *If you're so dumb that you don't insure what's important in life, you don't bloody deserve a second chance, do you?*

A remorse-filled sigh hissed out of him. Dumb wasn't the word of the day. Arrogance was. His greatest mortal sin, one he committed regularly and always against himself. Too bad it didn't reap the same pleasure as another mortal sin he was well on his way to hell for, the foolish coveting of a woman he didn't deserve.

It sliced his sorry soul to ribbons to say it, but—Callahan Woodworks was no more. Another sigh. Another cruel wrench at his heart, but aye. It was time to move on. His dream was gone. *Just like her...*

Even if she came back, Colby had made it abundantly clear she couldn't love him. The look in her eyes when he'd kissed her all those years ago had been quite the shock. He'd been so overcome, so blessed to have finally tasted the honey of her lips, that he'd actually taken a second or two to thank the Blessed Virgin for sending this particular angel into his sorry life, before he'd kissed Colby again.

Guess she hadn't felt the same. Her palm in

the center of his chest said it all. There was no need to follow it up with a stern, 'No.' But she had. Right before she turned her back on him and walked away.

He, one of Ireland's own sons, had the bad luck to fall in love with an American princess of royal, capitalistic birth. Only this one was not like the others he'd come across. Ah, no. Colby might look like a radiant model with those straight forward, piercing gold, tiger-eyes, but she was tough, as in bloody tough.

She played soccer for Boston's beleaguered women's team, the Storm. Her bitch-slapping aura tended to arrive at least a dozen steps ahead of her like the bow wave of an incoming destroyer. Not that the opposing team of female ruffians wasn't as brash. They just weren't—her.

The first time Ash had seen Colby on the field, her head up, her cocky don't-mess-with me chin tossed to the other players, Holy Mother of God, he'd gone weak in the knees like a little boy with his first crush. Smitten for the one woman he could never have.

Aye. An eejit to the bloody core. Lost me girl and all me dreams. What am I good for? Blimey, I need a beer.

Ash settled for a smoke instead before the

lonesome walk home. His fingers tugged the nearly flattened pack of cigarettes out of his shirt pocket, an automatic response to the hole in his heart. The night was late, and he'd already murdered one too many pints back at Shenanigan Rose, one of his favorite Boston pubs. He was beyond fluthered. And without a ride.

Cupping a hand to his mouth, Ash lit the Dunhill Fine Cut Black with a quick flash from his cheap lighter and sucked in a deep breath of nicotine. Not that the burning ember at his fingertips brought any comfort. Nothing did. Not his pints, nor the guys at the pub, nor a quick Ave down in the chapel at Sister Bernadette's Homeless Shelter. 'Twas as if Colby had taken the sun out of Boston when she'd left. Even his Guinness tasted—flat.

He'd come to town with Hammer tonight, both needing a hearty pint and a pick-me-up. Kev had begged off, too busy with the arsonist's evil deeds to join them. But Hammer left hours ago. Something about the missus and a sick little one, and like a rabbit with its tail on fire, he was gone.

There'd be no friendly ride back to Ash's flat tonight, just a good brisk walk that might clear his head if he didn't pass out on the way. Or stumble over his two big feet and dive head first into the drink. Back in County Mayo, he would've trudged into one of the many woods near his da's farm and crashed in the clover until the morning sun. But Southie sidewalks were harder than Irish meadows, and, while the neighborhood had improved, there were still pickpockets and panhandlers afoot. And worse.

Glory be, but last call had never presented such a dilemma. He couldn't even crawl into the spare back bedroom at Callahan Woodworks. Not tonight and never again. It was bloody well gone with his dreams and every last drop of the blood, sweat, and tears he'd put into the place. Aye, he'd bawled his eyes out somewhere between the second and fifth pint tonight. He might again. Could be why Hammer bugged out early. Nobody likes a blathering drunk. *But Jesus. I've really done it now.*

The randy rev of a motorcycle behind him jerked Ash's gaze from the harbor to the brightly lit street. *A Harley, huh?* Good-looking bike, not that he could afford one. That day was gone, but he lifted a hand to the leather-clad guy in the saddle just the same. The bike sounded punk, and that was simply what guys did. They acknowledged each other. Didn't need to know names for that.

For a second, the rider cocked his head, and Ash thought maybe he knew the guy. It could happen. The biker was a little dude, and something about his erect posture and squared, but petite shoulders rang a bell. Not that Ash's head wasn't already ringing. It'd been a month of Sundays since he'd been this hammered. Ha, that was nearly a funny joke, himself hammered when he should have been—ashed. *Aye. Funny. Nah.*

Bringing the Harley's front wheel to a sharp right and out of traffic, the biker headed straight for Ash. He breathed a tired groan, hoping his hand gestures hadn't been misconstrued as offensive. At this time of night, anything was possible, but he wasn't in the best condition for a round of fisticuffs. *Nah now, boyo. I'm wasted enough for the both of us. Drive that pretty little motor scooter home to yer mama and let me be.*

Apparently, the brash driver thought otherwise. Throwing his weight backward, he jumped the front tire of his bike over the curb and came to rest, blocking Ash's drunken stroll along Boston Harbor.

Ash dismissed the short pest with a flick of his hand. *Feck off.* He had nothing left in him to fight with or for.

But the little dude stuck both feet to the sidewalk. Interesting. He wore combat boots. Not the usual footgear for a biker, but whatever. Still straddling his bike, he unstrapped his helmet.

The tiny thing was probably Xtra small. Maybe XXtra-small like its owner. Ash grunted, clenching a fist, just in case. Little guy or not, nothing good happened in the wee hours, not in Ireland, Boston proper, nor Southie.

Tussled locks of gold spilled out from under that helmet. Might as well have kicked him in the balls. Ash grimaced at the sight, in actual physical pain. The day that started with his dearest dreams going up in flames had just gone from being really, really bad to a helluva lot worse. Mother Mary and sweet Baby Jesus, could it really be her?

"Colby Quaid?" he asked, sure he'd drunk himself silly and his Irish eyes were lying. Talk about his dearest dreams going up in smoke. The sight of this one come back to life nearly dropped him to his knees.

Ash didn't know whether to fall down on his face and thank heaven for her or stand there like a fool and just drink her in like the ghost she probably was. Where once he would've given his left nut just to turn her over his knee and wail on her ass with a wooden spoon for leaving him, now he was smitten as hard as the first time he'd seen her.

Love at first sight should nah hurt so much nor take so much from a man.

She stabbed her chin at him, as cocky as ever. Still as lovely as a morn in spring. "Ash. See you're still drinking."

"Aye," he breathed, slurring even that one word. And down he went.

What an ass. The first time I see him in years, he's falling-down-drunk. As usual.

Righting her bike, Colby shut it down before she scrambled over to help Ash. Cupping one hand under his hard head, she leaned into his face just as a hearty blast of alcohol vapor watered her eyes. *Guinness again.*

He looked good though, the laugh lines at the corners of his eyes relaxed and a half-smile on his handsome, though unconscious, face. Even passed out, the man was still drop dead gorgeous, but Ash was a genuine Irish lady-killer when sober. His face was finely boned, his nose slender and straight.

He'd cut his hair since the last time she'd seen him, so short there was nearly nothing left of it to run her fingers through—if she'd been so inclined. A couple days' scruff shadowed his prominent chin and jaw, and... damn him. He'd been smoking again. She could smell it on him, somewhere between the heady scent of the black stuff he loved to guzzle, and the spicy aftershave he swore made him irresistible to women. Still...

This was Ash Callahan. What was not to love?

"How's all that drinking working out for you tonight, big guy?" she asked, already knowing the answer he'd give her had he been conscious. He'd never admitted to being anything better than: *Fine, Lass, fine.* So even though he couldn't hear her, Colby set him straight for the umpteenth time. "You look awful." *Awful good.*

The ego of this man. From the first moment he'd elbowed his way through the mob at Nickerson Field to shake her sweaty hand after a winning game, he'd assumed she liked him. Problem was—she did. Right from the start. Ash was a rowdy Irish braggart, an over-the-top know-it-all, and a true alpha male. Just her type if ever she were inclined to admit she had one. There was a time she'd loved this loud-mouthed

Irishman—until he'd ruined everything by kissing her.

His brows were as thick as ever. The softest blue eyes lay beneath those thick, fluttering lashes. The blue eyes of a dreamer. That was Ash from head to foot. A true Irish rogue with stardust in his charming eyes and just as full of blarney.

His facial features were gentle for a man his age, the kind of a face that could turn wicked mean when riled. She'd only seen that side of him once when a bare-chested, face-painted fan plowed into her after a game and copped a feel. Ash nearly took the drunken guy apart.

He wasn't a mean drunk himself. Quite the opposite. He tended to think he was witty after a couple of pints. He also thought he could sing. His playlist? The old Irish American favorites, of course. "Irish Eyes", "Danny Boy", "The Minstrel Boy", every "Ave Maria" ever written, and a hundred Irish drinking songs, including the rowdy "Finnegan's Wake."

Brushing her fingertips over the stubble on his shaved skull, she located the knot on the back of his head. She'd had guys fall for her before, just not hard enough their heads bounced. She was fairly sure she'd heard Ash's when it hit the sidewalk. Not that it wasn't hard enough to dent concrete, but still. Her fingers came back slick. He was bleeding. *Oh Ash...*

Tugging his broad shoulders onto her lap, Colby cradled his head, debating whether to call his drinking buddies, Kevin and Hammer, and let them deal with him. Both were married. They were probably home with their families. And the hour was late...

Tugging her cell up from her jacket pocket, she used it for the first time in days to summon an Uber driver for her passed-out friend. Ash had a room at his shop. She could drop him off, tuck him in, give him a kiss on his forehead that he'd never remember, then face the music with her mum. *What a helluva welcome home.*

Colby used the time waiting for the Uber driver to remember. "Are you still a player?" she asked Ash, surprised at the longing in her voice.

Did she love this guy? Without a doubt. Would she ever tell him? Probably not. They lived in two different worlds, more so now that she'd been to war, and he'd been to—what? Party central at the pub while she'd been one? Yeah. She and he were not happening.

It'd been awhile since she'd held a man she cared for, which would be him. Only him. Tracing a fingertip over his plump bottom lip, she recalled their one and only kiss. He'd been surprisingly gentle, his mouth questing after hers, not storming in with no holds barred, but sweet, soft, and tasting of beer.

She licked her lips, remembering that their only kiss was the beginning of the end. She'd expected that passion and a rowdy Irish heat would've come with the kiss, not the tentative, questing claim of a poet nor the oh, so gentle reverence of a—a priest, for hell's sake. That wasn't what she'd needed at that time in her life, not with the oppressive weight of the mighty Quaid Empire looming over her future like the shadow of Death, complete with its sharpened scythe to slice the life out of all her dreams.

Hell, no. She'd wanted the same passion from that kiss that Ash carved his masterpieces with. The branding. The fire. She'd wanted his hands all over her and her name shouted to the rafters.

But what she'd gotten was a quick, sweet peck on the lips and a helluva lot of confusion. He'd pulled back from her mouth and bowed his forehead to her forehead, the ass. So why the hesitation back then? There'd been no one else in his life, so it wasn't as if he'd already given his heart away. She'd even sucked on a breath mint beforehand—in case.

But at the last moment, there on the edge of something that could've been, should've been, mind-blowing, he'd just pulled back and stopped. For certain, it wasn't because of her. No, it was him. Just him.

Ash had been unexpectedly timid. Shy. A surprise, that. She truly hadn't seen it coming, not from a party animal the likes of him. She'd expected... more. Especially as pumped full of adrenaline as she'd been after the game.

If there were a way, she'd go back in time, and before she'd left, she'd do him right. Oh, hell, she probably wouldn't have left at all once she'd kissed him like she'd wanted. With plenty of tongue and groping and... *that.* Maybe that would've set him on fire for her like she'd been for him ever since. And yet...

Running her fingers over his chin, Colby ended up cupping his jaw. Truth was... The timid, gentle kiss that night had scared the bejesus out of her. That was when she knew she had to leave before she couldn't.

But now, with him unaware and right where she wanted him, she closed the distance. Smoothing her hand to the nape of his neck, she lifted his head and pressed her mouth to his lips. Softly. Almost as reverently as he'd kissed her then, she kissed him now. Running her tongue over his bottom lip, she savored the masculine taste of him once more. Inhaling deeply, she drew the scent of the only man she'd ever loved back into her soul.

It wasn't enough.

Shocked at her nerve, her fingers now on his cheek, Colby pulled back. She had no right to kiss him like this, not after what she'd done to him. Life never gave you what you wanted, did it? Only what you needed. *Whoever said that was dumber than a box of rocks.*

Uber drivers were worth their weight in gold. It took too few minutes for one to show at the curb. It took a couple more to load Ash into the back seat and strap him in. Colby gave the driver the address to Callahan Woodworks, less than five miles away, intending to follow on her bike.

But the driver shook his head. "I cannot take him to this address."

She lifted a brow. "Why not?"

Her friendly driver, who looked like he might be from India or Pakistan, shrugged his shoulders. "I am sorry to be the one to tell you, but Callahan's burned to the ground today. There is nothing left. I saw it on the news."

Colby sucked in her shock. No wonder Ash was falling down drunk tonight. Callahan Woodworks was everything to him. He'd built his business and his name from the ground up after he'd left everything behind in Ireland.

Her fingers tapped against her thigh. *What to do? What to do?*

Simple. When in doubt, fall back on what you do best.

She had the driver take Ash to Beacon Hill.

CHAPTER FIVE

One eye to his pillow, Ash cracked his other open to the soft light of—somewhere that was not his flat. This pillow was clean and smelled of lavender and starch. Maybe even bleach. Aye, not his place at all. Flexing his elbows, he flattened both palms to the extra soft mattress, ready to get back on his feet.

Not happening. The room not only spun, it bucked, twisted, and rolled. He'd no more than lifted his head up from the pillow when he let it drop again. Maybe Hammer had taken him home to his place? That'd be a first, and it made sense, but no. Ash was almost one hundred percent sure Hammer had left the pub before he did last night. Something about...

Ah. He couldn't think, so he closed both eyes, content to rest until he puzzled this predicament out. He recalled last call, and, for some ungodly reason he couldn't fathom, a taxi ride. For sure, he'd had a couple smokes by the harbor. Hadn't he?

No matter. The pillow was soft and his head was hard and pounded like the devil. He stayed put. On his belly. Too knackered to care where he was.

"How is she?" Colby asked her mother's personal assistant, Tula White Feather, not her real name, but some hippie moniker she'd assumed years earlier. They stood in the hall outside her mother's room on the second level. The grand home on Beacon Hill was quiet. Colby had taken a quick shower and changed into a pair of faded denim jeans and a simple t-shirt, stalling the confrontation with her mother.

Tula hailed from the West Coast. She'd been part of the pot-smoking generation of the seventies and still wore the lifestyle. Dressed in a tie-dyed caftan, one she'd probably dyed herself with organic dyes of every color in the rainbow— you know the drill. Colby was fairly certain Tula had also smoked one too many bongs in her past life or had inhaled more tokes than she should have. For all her raging against the chemicals that Corporate America released into the environment on a daily basis, she had no trouble putting certain other chemicals, aka marijuana, in her system.

Tula tittered on a regular basis as if she thoroughly enjoyed her own company, answering her inquiries instead of letting Colby speak for herself. Ah, the seventies. Mus have been a rockin' good time.

"She's sleeping, Miss Colby, but you already knew that, didn't you?" Tula rolled her aquamarine eyes. "Yes, I'm sure you did. Have you traveled far to get here?"

Colby waited the space of a heartbeat for the answer that was sure to come.

"Of course, you did, child." Tula breathed a sigh. "What am I thinking? I'd hate for you to wake her up, though. She's restless these days.

She needs the sleep. Can I make you a sandwich? Some tea?"

Again, Colby waited as Tula's brightly colored zigs and zags swished around her broad hips when she turned down the hall. "Why, I'd be glad to fix breakfast, you know that. Do you take cream and sugar in your coffee?"

"Yes, ma'am," Colby got in a quick reply to what sounded like multiple-choice questions. "In my coffee. I don't drink tea." *Never have, never will.*

"Yes, you do, honey child. You certainly do." *Whatever that meant.*

Tula strolled down the generous staircase, one hand on the elegantly carved handrail, the other on her ample cleavage as if she had to hold onto her breasts for fear they'd get away from her when she walked. She did tend to bounce a little. Make that a lot. Another legacy from the burn-the-bra seventies.

Colby eyed the changes in the house she used to call home. A new Persian rug, this one of tan and cinnamon hues, covered the oak hardwood floor in the formal dining room at her left. A larger, more expansive chandelier hung over the solid oak dining table that stretched from one end of the massive room to the other, elongated to accompany a massive dinner feast. There was a day that table would've been filled, each chair too, and a lavish meal laid for all to partake. This old house had rung with importance, with music and parties, soirées and dances galore, but no more.

Dust clung to the spaces between each baluster of the staircase now. A cobweb dared stretch from one end of the crown molding in the grand entrance to the tip of the solid wood doorframe below it. The magnificently carved eagle over the door looked dingy and gray from dust and lack of attention. It used to shine with lemon oil polish, but then, her mother once employed a full staff of maids, butlers, and chauffeurs. How things changed.

"The war over yet?" Tula tossed over her shoulder, her caftan spread at her sides like wings. Colorful, laid back butterfly wings.

"Most likely not," Colby replied, following the woman into the kitchen.

"As I expected," Tula breathed. "Peace, child. What the world needs now is peace and love, sweet love. That's the only thing that will fix it."

Why did that sentiment sound like a television commercial?

Tula waved her hand to the breakfast nook in the north facing bay window, the only place where

Colby had ever felt comfortable. She'd always belonged to the blue-collar world more than to high society. Once upon a time the fishing boats in the harbor had pulled at her, the thrill of a close game of baseball, and ice skating races in winter. But soccer had won her heart. Always soccer.

Her world then had been filled with practice and bruises, but she'd proven herself, by hell. The day she'd startled her coach with an audacious keepie-uppie before she'd scored the winning goal and clenched state, went down in history. Did she get a good tongue-lashing for that cocky display? She would've been surprised if she hadn't, but she'd ruled the day, hadn't she? She'd won.

Was it worth her coach's displeasure to know she was *just that good*, that she'd known instinctively where the mid-fielders were and how much time was left on the clock? That she trusted her battle-honed skill as the league's best—in your face!—center striker? You bet your Irish ass the butt chewing was worth it. Her team and fans loved her spit-in-your-eye attitude as well as her win-or-die-trying game-ending plays.

But that plucky notoriety had come at a price. Her mother fought her every step of the way.

Why Bella ever got the notion that her only child would change from a sports jock into the prissy daughter-of-her-dreams in frilly dresses, Colby never knew. Not for certain. She'd just suspected. The emotional distance between them had to do with Colby being an unexpected and unplanned *bonus*, a child born too late in life to parents who were too busy and too single-minded to change their lifestyle. Yes, there'd been birthday parties and celebrations, but there'd never been—what was the word?—inclusion?

Born into wealth when one's parents were in their forties and already set in their ways, did not a happy ending make. At least not in the Quaid family. Which explained Colby's need to leave Boston behind and set out on her own. She'd been born a tomboy with grit in her eye and a cuss word on her tongue, not a silver spoon. She'd like to keep it that way.

The Army gave her what she'd desired most— herself. She had no one to answer to once she'd enlisted, except drill sergeants at first, then a couple commanding officers later in her career, most whom she respected. She'd fought to be that army-of-one and ended up being one of the first women Rangers. Was it worth it? She thought so.

Tula laid a pressed napkin on Colby's knee

even as she set a saucer and cup—of tea, mind you—front and center on Colby's placemat.

"I don't drink tea," she reminded her mother's space-cadet caregiver.

Tula's light-brown brows lifted in surprise. "Since when?"

Hell, this never gets old... Colby held her breath. *Wait for it.*

"Of course, you don't, child. My mistake." With a twitter and a swirl of neon rainbow, Tula lifted the saucer away. "Coffee. You're a coffee drinker. I know that. I'll be right back."

Colby cocked her elbow to the table, her chin cupped in her palm as she stared out the window. It seemed the mighty Quaid Empire was in disrepair on the home front, too. Like it or not, she might have to stay longer than she'd planned.

The lovely aroma of coffee beans in the grinder wafted through the air, filling Colby's nose with the hope of a better day. That illusion was followed by a thump and a hearty, "Where's me feckin' trousers?" from upstairs.

Great. Ash was awake.

CHAPTER SIX

A man shouldn't wake up in a strange house without his trousers nor underwear, not with the mother of all hangovers squeezing his skull like an egg, and a cracked egg at that. Bloody or not, the tender bump on the back of his head didn't bode well. He must've really been plowed last night, a rare event for a man of his stature in the drinking class.

Ash swung his feet to the floor, instantly dizzy but soldiering on, buck-naked or not. What a bizarre place was this? Most of the walls to this room were a bright, blaring white that hurt his eyes, except the one opposite from where he sat. Posters of all sizes filled that wall, most just splashes of color he couldn't make out because they were moving. Narrowing his gaze, he stretched his neck and leaned forward. Just a little. Just enough to see...

Aye. He recognized them now. Soccer posters, the lot of them, Boston's winning-est women's team. *The Storm.* Best of state. Best in the feckin' world as far as he was concerned.

I'm in Colby's room? How the bloody hell—?

A sharp rap hit the door, and he grabbed for the covers.

Man, he looks good. Ash's eyes were still full of sleep and the side of his face was wrinkled from laying on it. Still all angles and corners from that stout Irish chin to his muscle-packed chest. Ash acquired that powerful build not from working out at some gym, but from hauling his own lumber at his workshop. The man did everything the hard way, even unloading his truck, a rust bucket of an Army surplus five-ton, when orders came in at the dock and he couldn't wait for his distributors to deliver. Not that he needed a truck that size, but that was Ash. Always out to prove his was bigger.

"Ash," Colby said to the naked man in her old room, the one with the flustered light in his eyes and the sheet pulled tight across his hips. A silver crucifix suspended from a silver chain at his neck.

For whatever reason, he'd doffed his boxers some time during the night, if those bare hipbones meant what Colby suspected they meant. Long, hairy legs with knees spread braced the big guy at the edge of the bed. If he'd rested an elbow to his knee and cupped his chin, he could easily be mistaken for Rodin's *Thinker*. Until he opened his big mouth.

"This your room?" he asked, his head cocked and a salacious twinkle glimmering in his eyes. "You brought me here? On purpose, Lass?" Naturally, Ash used his other brain.

"I couldn't leave you on the street, could I?"

He had the nerve to wink, his index finger curled and beckoning her. "Come sit beside me then. We've got some catching up to be doin'."

"No. We don't." Colby shook her head to reinforce her answer to his come-on. "I'm only back in town to take care of family business, and you're only here" —she rolled her eyes over her room— "because I couldn't leave you passed out on the street. Nothing more."

"Ah, so now you're quoting Edgar Allen Poe to me." His brows arched in that devil-may-care-Tom-Selleck way. The man was no dummy, educated at some college in Dublin if she remembered right. But he came with a lot of nerve. He patted the mattress again, his head canted, and his offer—inviting. "Come sit down, Lass. You've got what you've always wanted, me in your bed for the first time."

The funny, over-confident clown hadn't changed a bit. He almost made her smile at his boyish charm amidst his audacious dare. But that day was past. She crossed her arms over her chest and stayed at the door. "Are you seeing stars?" *You should be.*

"Only when I look at you."

She'd worked hard to lose her Boston accent when she'd joined the Army. But he still relied on that lyrical Irish brogue that used to get to her every time. It worked. "I meant your hard head. It bounced on the sidewalk last night when you fell because you were drunk."

"Oh, that." Scowling, he reached to the back of his skull. Another wink and he skewered her with those rakish blue eyes. "What'd I do, heh? Fall for you again?"

Exactly. "Nope, sorry. You drank too much, and I just happened to be there when you keeled over. That was all."

A frown creased his brow in furrows that, just once, she'd like to trace with her fingertips. Maybe press a kiss there. She had yet to tap the real Ash Callahan, the one beneath the jovial mask. For all his teasing charm, she knew there was a dark side to his drinking. But that brogue... Ah, it got to her every time.

"Must've been a good night if I do nah remember it."

"You were knackered, Ash. Falling down drunk. It didn't look like a good night to me." *Talk to me. For once, stop the comedy routine.* The man had his devils just as she had hers. They'd just never gotten around to sharing.

Closing his eyes, he grunted at her, one of those *what-would-you-know-about-it-little-girl?* guy grunts. Ever the sexist. It was never that Ash hated women. He most definitely wasn't a misogynist, one of those arrogant types who considered themselves above women in all ways. Quite the opposite. If anything, Ash loved women in general. But like some cretin from the stone ages, his little brain had the entire female gender plugged into specific roles, none of them involving brains or skill.

She could've knocked him on his pretentious ass that day at Nickerson Field, when, in the midst of congratulating her win, he'd minimized her winning penalty kick with his next breath, bragging how they were *'still nah as tough as me boys in green'*, them *'boys in green'* being Ireland's national football team.

Well, no shit. We're not men, and we don't want to be! Don't you get it? There was and would always be a difference between men and women. That didn't make one gender better than the other. Colby respected the differences. She'd never aspired to be equal to any man. What woman in her right mind would?

"If I was drinking, 'twas only because..." He shut his mouth and looked at the floor, his thick bicep blocking her view as his hand skated over his head. "Aw, bloody hell."

He'd remembered his woodshop. She almost wished he hadn't.

Compassion for this rough and tumble man flared. There were times, she'd sensed that he was as lost in Boston—maybe the whole world—as she was. She couldn't blame him for drinking his sorrows away last night. He'd lost everything he'd worked so hard for. That was why he'd been on the street. He'd probably been the last to leave Shenanigan Rose. They might've had to throw him out.

"I'm sorry about your shop," she offered sincerely.

"Aye, well..." He ran that same hand over his face with a grumbly sigh, thumbing the sleep out of his eye socket. "Guess I'll be going."

"Stay," she said firmly. "You're hurt and—"

"And I do nah need your pity." That bark surprised her. He hadn't lifted his gaze from the floor. His pride was hurt, so he'd lashed out at her. That was all this was about. "Just tell me where you put me trousers, woman, and I'll be gone from your life and your bed."

That did it. Colby crossed the room to him, needing him to look at her. "That'll be the day I kick you out of my house when you're injured. Stay and eat breakfast with me. We can talk then."

"Nah," he shook his head, still avoiding eye contact. "Time for breakfast is past. I've got to talk to the bank, and Kevin's sending an investigator by what's left of the shop. I'm too busy to—"

"Kevin Hayden? He's fire chief now?" She knew

he'd been in line for that promotion. Good for him.

Ash's head bobbed, but he hadn't look at her yet, and she needed him to. They couldn't part like this, not again.

Colby reached out, her fingers nearly at his chin, when he stopped her. "Don't. I've lost enough, woman. I do nah need to be reminded how much."

Taking a seat at his side, she pulled her hand back. "I didn't mean to hurt you."

He waved her off with a dismissive grunt. "Just tell me where you put me clothes."

"Your shorts were on you when I left, but your jeans were dirty. I tossed them in the washer. They're drying now, so shut up and listen. You're not going anywhere until you've had breakfast, and I'm sure you're physically sound."

He met her gaze then, his blue eyes steel. "You were the one who undressed me then? What you going to do now, check to see if I'm man enough?"

Him being man enough was never their problem. "I could," she declared, her chin up. Not that she would physically check him, but she cared enough not to let this big-mouthed Irishman take off running the minute he lifted his drunken head from the pillow. "As for your shorts..." She pointed to the boxers on the floor at his feet, flustered that he was naked. "They're right where you left them."

He saw them then. "Aye. I remember now. I sleep better without them." As if he'd read her mind, the big cat flipped a switch and purred, grinning. Flexing his elbows, Ash flattened his palms to the mattress behind him, nodding at the sheet barely covering his hips as if telling her with his eyes: *You know you want it.*

If that sheet slipped any farther...

Colby swallowed, embarrassed she'd gotten into another tight squeeze with this player. Ash Callahan was vexation and charm rolled into one sexy man-package. She closed her eyes, not needing to gauge his reaction. She already knew. The covering over his—lap—had just tented, and she was on the verge of losing this battle of wills. She should've let him sitting there and run for her life. But she didn't.

"What am I going to do with you?" she asked, her voice as breathy as a schoolgirl's in the boy's locker room after a winning homecoming game.

A heavy hand branded her thigh. His fingers clenched, shooting a lightning bolt straight to her overheated core. Her nostrils flared at his signature scent, the wild blue sea with a splash of sawdust, tobacco, and beer. A hint of clean sweat. Manly scents she hadn't realized she'd craved until now. Ash was her meth and her poison, her good boy, bad boy, and her in-between boy. He was sin incarnate with his clothes on, but with them off?

Her pulse set to throbbing.

"If you're smart, you'll be kissing me again." His voice grated dangerously low, the firm weight of his hand setting the skin under her jeans ablaze.

Her heart kicked it up a notch, way past cruise control at the invitation. *Major Tom to ground control...*

But how could this thing between them work? They were opposites in every way, in social standing, future plans, and aspirations. Ash was the dreamer and the romantic. He was the guy who put stars in the sky, and she the realist, the combat-honed sniper who shot those same stars down like clay pigeons.

The last few years, she'd lived by sheer grit and determination, her competitive streak and paranoia her wingmen every step of the military way she'd set her boots to. The rose-tinted glasses that ninety-nine percent of all Americans like her wore, were long gone, traded in for wide-open eyes afraid to fall asleep in the dark. She'd done things in war she wasn't proud of, while he'd— what? Wiled his time away between pipe dreams, easy women, and bar tabs?

They hadn't a prayer of making it. Her primary goal was dismantling Quaid Corporations and to be gone from Boston as soon as she could, not to settle for less. And marriage was definitely less. Colby opted out of it the day she'd put Boston in her rearview.

Then there was the dilemma with her mother. Hell, she hadn't even spoken with Bella yet. This wasn't the time for closure or whatever Ash thought he needed.

"No," Colby meant to declare regular Army-style. Why it came out in a whisper, she didn't know.

CHAPTER SEVEN

Gods damn her! She'll nah do this to me again!

But there Colby sat at attention beside him, as tight as a soldier on sentry duty, her hackles up, and her lovely, toned body poised, no doubt, to break his nose if he stepped out of line. And she could do it, too.

Ah, but she was a vision of fierce, feminine perfection. Her blonde lashes were long and thick, so thick he ached to feel their sweet caress on his cheek. Dark amber eyes, more molten copper than honey at the moment, filled with tenderness, itself overshadowed by that dazzling bitch-slapping aura of hers. Did she think she needed to defend herself? From him? Jesus, Mary, and Joseph, nah. Never!

More than anything, Ash's arms yearned with a need so deep to shelter her from the very foes she ran headlong into. To hold her safe in his keeping, so no one could hurt her again. Always, he'd seen through her mask. There was a little girl hiding there, and he bloody well knew it. He just didn't know how to call Colby out of her shell, which was more like razor wire than a shell now that he thought about it.

The impulse to slap his forehead lifted out of nowhere. *What an idiot* he was to have fallen for a woman as fine as Colby. She had no use for him, and he knew it, not with her heart encased in invisible armor like it was, her gentle soul hidden beneath the tactical gear of a warrior princess. 'Twas never a day she hadn't unsettled him. The glib in his silver tongue turned to lead with this woman, and there was no explaining it.

Am I truly so desperate that I lose me bloody mind when she looks at me?

Simple answer? *Aye. I'm that desperate and more.*

But where had the blushing red gone from all that beautiful gold? She'd been a strawberry blonde the last time he'd seen her. He lifted a curl to his nose, needing to understand. "You've lost the roses in your hair," he murmured, pulling in every last hint of her flowery scent, savoring every last breath. "Where'd they go?"

She tossed that winner-take-all chin at him, tugging the curl out of his fingers as she did. "Too much desert sun will do that."

He slid one hand down her thigh to her knee and locked on for the ride. "There'll be no more desert for you, young lady."

Their banter seemed playful until...

Mother of God, I'm a man, nah a saint! A man driven by the fire that swallowed his livelihood, as well as the one sitting at his side, the one who should *want* to sit at his side. *Couldn't she be just a wee bit desperate for me, too?*

Like that last time, Ash lost his head and rushed Colby before she could dodge or deflect his advance. He caged her face between his hands to hold her, to keep her from running. Crushing his mouth to hers before she could analyze the life out of the feelings of his heart. Before she could hurt him.

Loving this woman should nah be so bloody difficult.

He'd anticipated her being defensive, maybe a little surprised at his passion, but it seemed as if he'd hit a brick wall instead of a beautiful woman. She didn't tilt backward as he'd expected. At least she hadn't slapped him, nor told him no again. He hated that word on her tongue.

Her tongue. Blimey. He hadn't expected her to part her lips as easily as she did and offer that succulent morsel as she had. He angled for deeper penetration, savoring the sassy taste that came with her. Her palm came gently to his cheek, but she didn't dig her fingernails in and scratch him, another sign he might be on the right track. For the first time, ever.

The warm, wet honey of her sweet mouth stirred the blood in his veins like a swizzle stick in a glass of Jack and Coke. A groan lifted up from his broken heart, tearing at his soul for all the losses he'd suffered, herself being the greatest. He couldn't kiss her long enough, deep enough, or sweetly enough. There'd been no other since she'd deserted him for the Army. He couldn't believe he was kissing her now, nor why she let him.

The sheet drifted out from between them as, slowly, Colby relaxed. The cold stiffness of a soldier softened into lush curves and warm breasts under his thundering chest. He meant to bed her now, if she'd let him. Did she just moan in his mouth?

He must've been doing something right, so Ash kept on with his doing. He dared let one hand curl around the nap of her neck—possessively—while the other cupped her thigh as a man should hold his woman. With pleasuring her until she screamed his name to the rafters on his mind, Ash tugged her backside fully onto the mattress, his lips still interlocked with hers. Pressing her flat to her back, he planted one knee at the edge of the bed and straddled her clothed thighs.

Fervently, he eased one hand under her shirt and palmed her warm belly, skin to skin, thrilled at the silky softness of her skin. The glorious feminine heat. There was no other explanation, either he was on fire or she was. He leaned over her, finally sheltering her, his instincts emboldened and the tip of his staff on target.

All at one, her palm flattened against his breastbone, exerting pressure. "Your heart's pounding," she breathed into his mouth.

"Aye, Lass. Like always. For you," he mumbled, that same heart climbing up his throat.

She ran her tongue over his teeth, and bit his bottom lip, offering hope with her customary edge. The tease. She couldn't just accept him for the love he intended to give her. Nah, there always had to be a struggle with Colby. A contest of wills.

So be it.

He endured the barrier her hand had just created as he poured his soul into her open mouth, using it as a funnel to channel his desires, wanting them to be her desires, too. That was what could make a match, them both so hungry and horny for each other they were willing to lose themselves to make the other whole.

With a breathy sigh, she turned her face, breaking the contact and crushing him once more. "We're so different."

Aye, that meant she was wealthy and didn't need Ash providing for her. Well, two pigs and a pence, he didn't care. He *would* be her man, and he would provide for her... somehow...some way. A man took care of his woman. He would!

"No, we're nah," he insisted, but before he could finish his thought—

"Yes, Ash. We are."

His forehead sank to her temple, his foolish nose flaring to draw in her scent before she pulled completely away. To remember the smell of her hair before he lost it again. "I can nah make you love me if you don't want to," he rasped, his heart crushed. "The Lord knows I've tried."

She said nothing, just lay there panting, her hand still on his pounding chest, her fingers spread wide. He lifted his hand from her hip to cover her fingers. "I have nah riches nor trinkets to give you. You know that. I can't pave your streets with gold now, nor will I ever be able to." Ash licked his lips, wishing she'd look at him. "Those things were never meant for me, but I can promise you one thing."

She faced him then. "I never wanted *things*. Don't you get it? That was why I left Boston in the first place. All those *things* cluttered up my life. The expectations. And not just from my mother."

Ah, Glory be. She didn't want to know what that one thing was that he could promise her. Typical Colby. Always on the offensive. Never seeing what was in front of her pretty nose. Always ready to run. That stubborn streak might've won her soccer trophies, but he was bloody tired of the chase.

Letting her go, Ash leaned back on his haunches, and dragged a hand over his still pounding and very stupid head. *Here we go again.* "Go on, tell me. What did I expect from you that was nigh impossible for you to live with?"

A grunt vibrated deep from her belly. "You don't want *me*, Ash. You never did. You want some simpering female, preferably barefoot and pregnant, doting on your every word and making eyes at you for the rest of your life. You want someone who's content to wait at home for you at the end of the day with a big pot of Irish stew and homemade bread. Right?"

He loved the way her brows slanted in anger, but she was wrong. Sort of. What man didn't want his woman waiting for him at the end of a hard workday, maybe with a beer in one hand and her clothes in the other? Wasn't that a woman's place in the world, to want to please her man in every way? To keep his house tidy, to raise their babies, and bake, and—all that other womanly stuff?

Clearing his throat, he said, "Aye, I get it. You think I'm old fashioned."

"You are." Her chin stuck out at him with those two words. "This isn't Ireland, Ash, and I'm not your mother. I'm not my mother, either. Nor her darling, perfect daughter." With that, Colby put both feet on the floor, her palms on her knees, and her eyes on the carpet, creating more distance between them.

What does me mum have to do with anything? Ash rolled a hand over his hard head, striving to understand. *Could Colby be right? Is that what I'm doing? Trying to fit her into the roles I grew up with?*

Trying to make her me mum? A shiver ran through him at that perverse thought. Boys did love their mothers, but not like—*that.*

He yanked the sheet over his thoroughly deflated ego. As liberated as American women claimed to be, he knew there were some who were exactly like his mother. He scratched his head, hoping he said the right thing next. "I don't want to change you. I like you just the way you are." Why couldn't she see that?

"Is that right?" She cocked an evil eye. "Then what do you see me doing ten years from now?" She snapped her fingers. "Come on, Ash, think fast. Tell me. Now."

"Umm." He had nothing but that fire-in-the-hearth dream rattling around in his head, but he was smart enough not to lead with it.

Her fingers snapped in his face again. "Spit it out. What am I doing in ten years? Baking? Washing *your* clothes? Darning *your* tattered socks?"

Holy Mother of God, she made those simple acts of kindness sound like something no woman in her right mind would want to do. "You're putting a lot of pressure on me." Another swipe over his head, but—she was right. He had pictured her pregnant with his son, maybe sons, waiting at home for him. Only she'd been happy to be there. She'd even had stars in her eyes—in his dreams.

When she expelled a huff through her flared nostrils, followed by a guy kind of a snort, he blurted, "I see you doing whatever you want to be doing, darlin'." There. That ought to make him a few points.

Colby cocked her head, still glaring through narrowed eyes.

Jesus, Mary, and Joseph, if there was a more obstinate woman on earth, he didn't know her.

"And that would be?"

Flummoxed again—until he recalled that sporty motorcycle she'd ridden into town. "Nah sure." Ash pinched his brows and his lips, going for a thoughtful expression. "I doubt you're much of a mechanic. Motocross maybe?"

That earned him a pair of raised brows as if he'd maybe answered correctly, not his forte. But it could've just happened. He swallowed hard and waved his hand in an arc over their heads. "I can see it now. Callahan and Quaid. The greatest—"

The frown again. "Callahan and Quaid? What's that about?"

What else? He shrugged, proud of his woman. "I'd be your manager."

Chuffing, she pushed to her feet. "See what I mean? You Tarzan, but me not Jane." Colby didn't turn until she was halfway out the door, but then it was just to toss another evil glare his way as she hissed, "Get a clue, Ash. Get a gawddamned clue."

CHAPTER EIGHT

Leaving her room and the egotistical scoundrel in it behind, Colby beelined to her mother's, a palatial suite all in itself, complete with a lavish sitting area looking out over Boston Commons. The door was cracked, so she peeked in.

"Colby!" her mother gushed. Still in bed with her hair in her traditional, but stylishly chic turban, Bella Quaid waved her forward. "Come here. Where have you been? It's been far too long since..." One brow spiked. "You're not still in the Army, are you?"

Colby embraced her mother, instantly aware of how frail Bella was since the last time she'd seen her. "No, Mom. I'm out." *Unless they activate me again.*

"It's about time." Bella smoothed the quilted silk coverlet over her lap. It matched the powder blue of her turban, as did the bed jacket buttoned up to her chin. "Stay awhile. When did you get here?"

Taking her place at the end of the bed, Colby startled at the physical change in her mother. Wiry gray hairs peeked out from beneath the turban instead of the dark auburn of a woman who'd once valued physical beauty. Her brows hadn't been plucked recently, and an actual mustache, faint but still there, graced her upper lip. Age spots speckled her cheekbones like muddy smudges cast off from a spinning dirt bike wheel. Most telling of all, Bella wore no crimson lipstick, her trademark.

"Power," she'd once told Colby. *"Red is a power color. Wear it well, and it will open doors."* That was one motherly lesson Colby had actually taken to heart, though her power color was more blood red than cherry red and had always been earned the hard way.

"I arrived late last night. Tula and I have kept

in touch" —since you refused to— "and I needed to check in to see things for myself." Colby wouldn't have been there now if not for Tula's concise message to come home.

A coy smile lit Bella's tired amber eyes. "Aw, you came back to see me. Just me." She made it sound as if Colby's being there was a special treat.

"Of course. I've been worried about you. What's happened since I've been gone?"

The coy act faded as if a switch were flipped. "You've got a boy in the house, don't you? That's why you're here. You're lying, aren't you?"

The same old accusations...

Colby let a slow breath hiss out between pursed lips. She never understood her mother's out-of-the-blue jumps to unfounded conclusions. Bella must have led one helluva rowdy life as a teenager, the standard she'd set and obviously still judged Colby by. Perhaps she had sneaked boys into her room when she was a youngster, but Colby'd always had better sense. She'd never brought a boy home when she'd lived here, and oddly—she glanced over her shoulder—that sexy beast in her bedroom this morning was the first.

Wasn't that a startling revelation? Or admission. Or whatever the hell it was? In so many ways, Ash had been first. Her first real crush. Her first heartthrob. The first and only man she'd wanted to settle down with once upon a damned long time ago. Now that she'd made that clear as mud, at least in her mind—

"Actually, yes. Ash Callahan is staying here until—"

"You can't be serious! That good-for-nothing Mick's here? In my home?" A self-righteous head tilt stiffened Bella's long neck. Ah, the wrinkles. The crepey skin. More telltale signs of her mortality slipping away. "How could you do something like that behind my back? Or God's sake, he's... he's Irish!"

Colby rolled a shoulder, hating the continual battle of wills with her bigoted, outspoken mother whose ancestors had come from Britain, but still. That was generations ago. *What'd the Irish ever do to you?* "He stays, Mom. I'm not arguing, and I'm not asking. Ash is a good friend and—"

"Why him?" Another hiss. Another benchmark Colby couldn't jump high enough to meet. She'd never dated the popular, wealthy Boston boys her mother would've preferred. Perhaps that was what had drawn her to Ash in the first place, her need to oppose Bella in all things. To blaze her own way in her pretentious world.

Like it or not, there was a stark difference between a self-made man and the privileged boys born into old money in Boston, the ones who didn't sweat or know how to make something of themselves without Mommy and Daddy's help.

Ash was the proverbial bad boy: Irish, poor, and bloody proud of it. He might not fit the socially acceptable category of Boston's elite, and everyone within the sound of his voice knew he wasn't politically correct. But to be honest, that was part of his rowdy charm. He relied on none of the whitewash, glamour, or double-talk of the upper crust. He'd always known what he stood for, even back when Colby was still figuring her way out of Boston. Back when he'd decided he'd wanted her. Before she knew she wanted him.

She changed the subject. It was either that or dwell on the puzzle that was Ash Callahan, and that was just—confusing. The man was, annoyingly, not as transparent as she'd once thought. "I'd like to meet the Quaid board of directors, Mother. Can you arrange that or should I ask Tula?"

For a woman supposedly declining into Alzheimer's, Bella was unexpectedly lucid this morning. Perhaps the extra sleep had something to do with the way she lowered her chin into her high-buttoned collar and peered intelligently through her shaggy brows at Colby. "Why?"

"Because it's time I got involved in running the company. Is Mitch still handling everything?" *I hope so. That will make divestiture, if that's what it's called, easier.*

The strategy in talking with Bella was to keep the ball rolling. Any lag in dialogue invited opinions Colby didn't want to hear. Mitch Rhoades, her father's friend and trusted Chairman of the Board over all Quaid operations, might've been the better person to have had this conversation with, but Colby didn't intend to lie or beat around the bush with her mother. If Bella wasn't well, someone strong needed to make decisions.

"Where is he?"

"Who? Mitch?"

"That boy..." Bella folded her hands in front of her, interlocking her fingers, her eyes hard as steel. "Is he hiding in your room again?"

Right on cue, the jaunty Irishman himself walked past her mother's bedroom. Leaning backward, he did an impressive double-take with a twinkle in his blue eyes that Colby couldn't miss. Despite their failed attempt at *discussion*, there was a definite bounce to his step. He nodded to her but addressed her mother. "Good day to you, Mrs. Quaid. You're looking a might spry this morning."

Darned if Bella didn't pat her turban as if she'd been complimented. "I am spry, young man, and don't you forget it." She rolled one shoulder. "Are you sneaking around behind my back with my daughter? Confess and I'll go easy on you."

A roguish smile curved Ash's lips. The silver-tongued Irishman had just come up against the sharp-tongued lady of the house. Colby pressed her palms to the bed behind her, ready to watch the sparks fly.

How he could be in such high spirits after losing his business to a fire was no small thing. And therein lay one of the many differences between them. Ash was born with nothing but a lifetime of sweat, tears, and hard work in store for him. Yet he was the one who knew how to throw back and party with his friends down at the pub. Now he acted as if there'd been no close encounter between them, much less her harsh words.

Colby's life had been quite the opposite, full of privilege and wealth. She'd never wanted for anything until she'd left her pretentious life behind for the hard knocks of the Army. Why had she done that? Simple. The prospect of a life of leisure didn't entice her then or now. She didn't want doors held open for her to glide through, nor the rough ways smoothed over and the squeaky wheels greased until all she had to do was mention her name to have everything handed to her. Where was the sweaty fight to hard earned victory in that? The gut-busting joy at the end of the field in the winning goal?

Soccer was her first way out of the Quaid dynasty, but the Army offered the complete lifestyle change she'd craved. Nothing felt better than the day she'd traded her name brand jersey for olive drab.

The top brass had known precisely what they were getting when she'd enlisted. They knew who she was, but she'd held them to every line of her contract. More than anything, she'd fought to be one of their best grunts, to be capable all by herself. To be that damned army of one. To them it might've been just a glib sales pitch, but it was her chance at a real life. *Her life.* She'd earned every last ribbon, badge, and stripe—the hard way.

"Ah, you've wounded me heart. Would I sneak behind the back of such a fine lady as yourself,

Mrs. Quaid?" Ash asked, his brows raised in mischief. "Never, ma'am. I was just wondering if you might have a few pieces of paper I could sketch me new building plans on. Maybe a pencil or two."

Building plans?

"What could you possibly afford to build in this town?" Bella's tone of superiority was enough to gall a horse.

But Colby had to wonder. *You haven't any money to start over again, do you Ash?*

Damned if the cocky guy didn't invite himself into Bella's suite to stand politely at her bedside as if he were her servant instead of a guest. "Ah, but you see, I'll need a new warehouse for me business, and I have a solid plan. Me last place burned to the ground yesterday. You might've heard that sad story on the news, but the problem with that building was it belonged to someone else before I bought it. It was old and some of the inside partitions were already falling apart. But this one will be built to me specifications. 'Twill be all mine and 'twill be spacious enough for the pallets of all me woods on one side, the filled customer orders on the opposite side." His eyes glowed with excitement. "If I can get enough financial backing, I'll build an apartment in the rear of it or the days I work late. I'm nah against sleeping over and working hard if it keeps me customers happy."

Colby stifled a snort. *So that's what he wants. Money. What a jerk.*

Bella's fingers fluttered on her lips. "My husband used to sleep over on the jobsite when we were first married. When it was too late to drive home."

He did? Colby didn't know that.

Her mother turned a shy shrug at Ash. "And sometimes..." She giggled. "I stayed overnight with him. It was quite fun sleeping in sleeping bags, maybe on the floor of his office, but sometimes in a tent, with Burton."

"Ah, you are an adventurous lady," Ash teased. "I see where your daughter comes by it. 'Tis a noble trait for an explorer. Next thing you'll be telling me you danced naked in the moonlight and went skinny dipping."

Another shy giggle and—Bella blushed? Colby could only stare at the clever man romancing her mother. *Who ARE you?*

CHAPTER NINE

He could feel Colby's amber eyes drilling into him like a laser, but she'd had her chance. Now was his time to charm her mum. "You must be proud of your wee Colleen," he said, hoping for an in with someone—anyone in this proud, cantankerous family. "Seeing as she won state as often as she did—"

He caught a glimpse of Colby shaking her head out of the corner of his eye, but his big mouth kept going. "And to have a true American hero in your family, one of the Army's first female Rangers. Sweet Jesus, you must be proud."

Bella's mood turned sour, her face along with it. "Why should I be?"

Colby's lashes fell, but Ash couldn't believe it. "Nah proud?" he asked. "Of your daughter or of—"

"She defied me then and she defies me still!" Bella shrieked, stabbing a finger at said daughter. "Look at her. Why should I be proud of her? All she's ever done is leave me behind? Me! Her mother and the only one who ever loved her!"

That would've been a good time to leave, but the poor woman's bony fingers clenched the edge of her blanket as if she were holding onto a life preserver on the Titanic. Her skin was so thin he could see her pulse pounding at the hollow of her wrinkled neck.

Ash dropped to a knee at her bedside, not wanting her upset. "Nah proud of your only child, Mum?" he asked gently. "I'm afraid I don't understand. She means everything to you; I know she does. I can see it in your lovely eyes. It sparkles like the first stars of evening. And you mean everything to her. You're her mum. That's the way it works between *máthairs* and their wee ones."

Colby jumped to her feet, shaking her head. "No, Ash. It's not that—"

"But I've been so scared for her." Bella's anger dissolved into tears. "And she's been so naughty. She takes chances, and she comes home injured, and..." Bella lifted one hand to her mouth and whispered, "I'm afraid I've let her run wild. I should've taken her in hand years ago. She needs a good spanking is what she needs."

Ash would've grinned and agreed if he hadn't already known that would set Colby forever against him. "There, there," he offered instead, not risking even the tiniest glance at the tension-filled woman standing at the end of the bed.

Bella cocked her head at him, her eyes narrowed, looking down her elegant nose at him like one of his sternest Catholic nuns from school. "I'm sorry, but what did you say your name was?"

"Ash Callahan, ma'am," he said politely, daring to take hold of both her frail hands in his. Garish blue veins etched the backs of them, and the knuckles on her long slender fingers were knotted with arthritis. The poor dear was as cold as ice. "There now, be at peace, Mum. She's come home to you, and there's no need to be afraid for your daughter," he soothed as he clasped her fingers gently to warm them in his larger hands. "You should be proud. You raised a fine, strong woman who's come home to stand by your side because she loves you. That's the only reason she's here. Do you not see that?"

More tears and an awkward silence followed. Bella gulped. What's an Irishman to do, but fill in the gap? "That's children for you, isn't it, Mum? They want to spread their wings and fly, but we want to keep them safe in the nest, don't we? I believe 'tis only natural and right. That's what makes a good mother, the instinct to protect what's yours, is it nah?"

He could swear Colby's eyes were burning a hole into the side of his head, but what could he do? Leave her poor mother alone and distraught? He hadn't the heart for it.

"I don't know what you're talking about, but you've got the bluest eyes of any man I've ever known," Bella gushed, untangling one hand from his grip to cup his chin. "Look how handsome you are. Just like my Burton." She ducked her neck into her shoulders. Her brows lifted. "Burton and I used to do the most scandalous things at his construction sites after the crews went home. One time we went skinny dipping in the water barrel. We nearly got caught, and it was such fun!"

Ash couldn't hold back a grin at that secret she'd no doubt carried a long time. "Do I see a wee little bit of the devil in your pretty eyes, too?"

"Maybe," she chuckled. "I think you and me need to get better acquainted, Mr. Callahan. You're quite the catch." She turned her cheek to him, inviting a kiss.

Colby lifted a fist to her mouth and coughed. "It's time to go. Mom needs her rest."

Ash lifted his gaze from mother to daughter, very much inclined to kiss the charming, elderly Quaid. Bella needed that offering as much as her darling daughter. Only Bella was brave—or perhaps a tiny bit addled—enough to admit it.

"You're right," he said to Colby. Then he pressed a chaste kiss to Bella's cheek as he murmured, "I'll be back later to check on you, Mum. Is there anything you'll be needing while I'm gone? I'd be glad to get it for you."

Sweet Bella Quaid batted her lashes like the debutante she was and would always be. "A brandy would be nice," she purred, a suggestive glint in those rheumy eyes that had no doubt seen the world change during her lifetime.

He pressed a son's kiss to the back of her hand, smart enough to know that Colby had just turned her back on him with a curt, "I'll send Tula up, Mom. Take a nap. See you later."

Bella lifted one hand to the cheek he'd just

kissed and fluttered her fingers. "Promise you won't stay away too long."

What could he say but, "Yes, ma'am. I promise"?

That earned him a breathy, "Bah-bye."

An interesting turn of events. Ash strode out the door behind Colby, feeling as if he'd made at least one woman in the household feel good about herself. Little did he know...

"What were you doing in there?" Colby hissed, her finger in his face and her beautiful amber eyes throwing orange sparks that did nothing to dampen his spirits.

He nodded back at her mother's closed door. "Treating your mum with some respect," he replied simply. "She's failing, isn't she?"

"What was your first clue?"

"Jesus, woman! Why are you so mad at me all the blessed time?" It wasn't as if he'd weaseled his way into her poor mother's heart for the sake of a loan or anything. Ah, but that might be precisely what Colby thought, that he'd only talked about his new business to set her mother up for a handout. "You don't," he hissed.

"I don't what?" she shot back at him. "Think you're up to no good? When haven't you been?"

"I'd never!" he volleyed right back at her. "Your mum's nah a well woman, and she needs her daughter's support, but if you're so—"

"I'm not!"

"Blimey woman, will you let me finish? I don't need money that bad, and even if I did, I would nah take advantage of a sickly woman. The nerve of you!"

Colby opened her mouth but shut it as quickly. She took a deep breath. "What are you talking about?"

He wasn't so sure. "You do nah think I was trying to shill your mum? I wouldn't do that, you know. Nah to your mum nor anyone else's mum. Holy Mother of God, not to anyone!'"

The most bewildered maple-colored eyes stared back at him, brimmed with tears he hadn't seen coming. Ah, this woman was breaking his heart.

"I never thought you were, Ash. It's not that," Colby choked. "It's just that... I only came home to dissolve Quaid, Inc. I refuse to take over the family business, b-but.." Her index finger stabbed at the closed door behind them. "She never told me she was worried about me, not once. All those times I came home hurt. All this time I thought... I thought..." Her stomach lurched with a sob.

And Ash praised every last one of his Catholic Saints. His Colby was—crying?

CHAPTER TEN

Enough! Colby dashed a quick hand over her traitorous eyes and slapped on her Mean Bitch mask, the one that had gotten her through boot camp, combat, and one helluva lot tougher times than this. She swallowed her fears and faced her deadliest opponent, the man she now knew without a doubt, loved her. Ash had been so tender with her mother, heartbreakingly so. A man with kindness running that deep through him could hurt her, but she wouldn't stand for it.

"Do you have any paper?" he asked out of the

blue, slapping his chest like he was feeling for a pocket. "A couple of pencils wouldn't hurt, either. Maybe a good eraser. I've none on me."

"In my desk drawer." She pointed him to her bedroom.

Yes, he was puzzled at what had just taken place with her mother, well, so the hell was Colby. Never had she expected that confession of concern from Bella. Her head spun with the revelation that maybe, just maybe, she'd misinterpreted her mother's overbearing personality and sniping remarks all these years. "I kept a ream of printer paper in the bottom drawer when I lived here. Take what you need." *And go before I fall apart and make a bigger fool of myself.*

He nodded, his eyes so full of concern that she wanted to scream. "Your mum needs you," he offered calmly. "Would it be okay if I chatted with her later today? If I'm here, I mean. I will nah step on your toes if you do nah want me to see her again."

What could she say? She wasn't *that* cruel. "I don't care if you do or not." That came out meaner than she'd intended. "It's just that... all these years..." Her pride caught in her throat. "Mom never told me she was worried about me, and I... I..." *I thought she hated me.*

His gaze narrowed. "Parents have funny ways of telling us they love us, Lass. Me da used to whip me stubborn ass, and the whole time he was doin' it, he'd be telling me 'twas because he loved me. Even over me screeching me lungs out at 'im to lay off, he kept a-pounding me backside, and I kept a-screaming. But to this day, I have no doubt he loved me."

A choked chuckle burst out of her at that comical picture: Ash bent over his dad's knee, getting his ass whipped. He must've been a hellion as a boy.

Damned if he didn't wrangle a big, warm arm around her, and damned if she didn't let him. "Would you like to see what I've got in mind for me warehouse now that we both know who's nah going to be loaning me the cash to build it?"

Colby swallowed her pride. "I can't. There are too many things unsettled. I need to get another doctor in to assess Mom's condition. Tula thought Alzheimer's, but after seeing her like this, I'm not so sure. And I've got to talk with my father's friend, Mitch Rhoades, and I've got other" —for lack of a better word— "stuff to do."

"Ah, your board of directors guy."

"How'd you know him?"

"I went looking for me trousers, and..." He did a smooth Vanna White impression, gesturing over his chest and down his thighs. For the first time, Colby noticed the freshly washed jeans and gray Henley she'd laundered for him—like some doting woman. Ah, she'd done exactly what she'd always declared she wouldn't. But damn. The man did clean up fine.

"Your maid told me his name. Tula and I had a spot of tea after you left me with nothing but me underwear this morning. She likes to talk, does she nah?"

Colby leaned into the powerful frame at her side, her hackles lowered, and for once, enjoying the strength of Ash. "She also likes to answer her own questions and thinks she knows better than you."

Ash steered Colby toward the staircase. "You go take care of your business then, and I'll take care of mine. Sound good?"

"I might be a while. Are you going to...?" How does one eat humble pie? She tried again. "Will you be here when I get back?"

He had the nerve to wink. "You didn't scare me off this morning, darlin', if that's what you're asking. I'll be here, but I won't be keeping the hearth fires burning, nor will I be baking your bread, if that's all you think I'm good for."

She nearly laughed. He'd just thrown her words back at her without one hint of the in-your-face sarcasm she'd used.

He landed a hard smack to her ass with a growly, "Go on, now. Be off with you."

Damn him. That male chauvinist spank made her... smile.

Ash turned on his heel before he did something dumber than smacking Colby's sweet backside—like kissing it. Back in her bedroom, he made the bed and straightened the pillows, just to keep on the friendly side of his woman. He capped the shampoo bottle in her girly bathroom, so she wouldn't think he was a complete freeloader or a slob. When everything looked neat and in its place, he settled in the leather office chair at her masterpiece of a solid oak, roll-top desk.

Saints be praised, the haves in this world surely had it better than the have-nots. He stroked the honey-gold grain of what had to be the prettiest white oak he'd laid eyes on in years. An antique, the high gloss finish protected it well.

One of the cubbyhole drawers was a tad tight opening, but a spritz of wax could cure that.

He opened the pencil drawer, intending on borrowing two—until he spied his name written in the center of a flowery heart.

"What have we here?" What was he supposed to do, pretend he hadn't seen it? Uh-uh, no way. This little masterpiece deserved its due praise. He pulled the decorated tablet out, just for a quick look-see, mind you.

Glory be to God, the Father, Son, *and* the Holy Ghost. Maybe to Saint Michael, too. The inside cover was one big mosaic doodle of *Ash Callahans*, some written in exquisitely feminine cursive, some in variations of print, some sideways, and others upside down. These were not the doodling of some lovesick high school crush. The subject matter on those narrow-lined pages was bloody college calculus. Though few they'd been, he recognized some of the formulas from his own school days.

Leaning back in Colby's chair, Ash took his time leafing through her little secret cache. That woman of his was as intelligent and creative as she was beautiful. The more he studied the fine art mingled with formulas as long as the pages, he had to wonder. Why should an intelligent woman like her not want her due place in the world? It was rightful. He could see it now. Why hold her back?

Had that been what her stint in the Army was about? Her searching for the recognition she hadn't received at home? Was that what had fed her competitive spirit? What pushed her? Her need to be recognized for her true worth?

"I think I'm finally seeing you now, Lass," he muttered to himself as he licked his thumb and turned another page. One by one, the creations on each well-inked sheet of narrow-lined paper made him smile. She'd scrawled and decorated lavish curlicued vines and leaves, other hearts, but only two names. Always his. Always hers. Ash and Colby. Colby and Ash.

There were so many facets to the woman he loved, and, like a diamond, she shone in every one. Her soccer and military careers were just two of many sides. Yet she puzzled him. She'd said she intended to dissolve her father's business, yet that business seemed precisely her cup of tea. Colby definitely had the skills, the razor-sharp business sense, and she was the strongest woman on earth, of that he was quite sure. Why did she not take the helm and steer Quaid, Inc. into greater heights of financial success? Why not be the daring woman she was meant to be, since—by all the holy saints in heaven above—she already was?

Ash grunted at the paradox that was his Colby. Soft and sweet. Hard as nails. Yet, she seemed perpetually tossed on some storm sea, at least in her mind, as if she were not ready or willing to settle. Worse, as if she didn't know where to settle. Was it the freedom of the road that truly called her, or was it fear, maybe of failure, that had kept her running far from home? Ash planned to find out.

He did eventually locate the printer paper, and he replaced the tablet in the same place he'd found it, but saints be praised. The things Colby had left behind when she'd chased after her Army dream puzzled him. He had half a mind to keep on snooping, but no. He'd wait until she chose to share her heart. For the time being, it was nigh enough to know...

She loves me.

Chapter Eleven

Mitchell Rhoades. Black. Sixty something. Built like an NFL linebacker. Silver-haired and nearly as silver-tongued as Ash. Also, Burton Quaid's dearest friend and the best man for the job of running Quaid, Inc. The construction company founded by her father in the mid-eighties. It had spread across the world and was responsible for some of the tallest buildings on record.

Mitch had already wowed, as in completely overwhelmed Colby with detailed lists of corporate assets: Tangible, intangible, and personal. She was astounded to learn her company owned a long list of other corporations. Between them, all the investments, and the burgeoning accounts—mindboggling.

"And now for the liabilities," Mitch said as evenly as he'd reported the assets. Offering another portfolio, this one as thick as the other, he didn't wink nor patronize. If anything, he treated her as if she knew exactly what he was talking about—which she didn't.

Colby raised her hand at that point, unwilling to pretend anymore. "That's not necessary. Just tell me how I begin corporate dissolution, or if it's even possible." Her head spun with all the legalese he'd been throwing at her.

Mitch steepled his fingers to his chin. "May I ask why you're considering dissolving *your* company?" Emphasis on *your*...

"To be honest, it's a burden," she replied, shifting in her plush leather chair. "I have no intention of spending the rest of my life—"

"Being rich?" he bit out. It was startling how easily he'd morphed from fatherly to stern taskmaster.

She tossed her chin, not going to be bullied. *Many have tried. Damned few succeeded.* "It's not that—"

"Then what is it? Being the lead innovator in

the building industry? Building affordable housing in even the most inhabitable places in the world? Leveraging human need against incomparable balance sheets? What exactly is it about Quaid, Incorporated that you dislike?"

Not exactly what she meant, but okay. If that made this go down easier, let's do it his way. Colby leaned forward, into the fight. "You have to understand. I'm not my dad, and Mom's no longer able to manage business affairs. I have a life, Mitch, and I don't intend to spend the rest of it behind a desk." She'd almost said *waste the rest of it,* but caught her insult in time.

"Who asked you to?" Mitch didn't back down an inch. Just as she'd done, he leaned into what had become an intensely uncomfortable dialogue. "Just so we're on the same page, Miss Quaid, Bella hasn't managed the company for years. To be honest, I was looking forward to you taking the reins. You have your father's heart for this business. You have his eye."

She forced a swallow at that compliment. "His eye?" What the hell did that mean?

"You have his vision, Colby." He'd just gone from formal to personal, a ploy she recognized for what it was: Good business sense and a bull's eye hit below the belt. *Way to go, Mitch.*

"You might not realize it, but Burton saw beyond the hubris of the world. Yes, making money was important, but that wasn't why he founded Quaid, Inc. Did you ever travel with him?"

She shook her head. "I was busy."

"Ah, yes. Soccer. The Storm. I remember." He hadn't taken his eyes off of her. "You took state three years in a row in high school. At the same time, you were accepted by three notable universities. Yet you declined every offer and attended a community college. Instead of following in your father's shoes, you joined the Army and went to war." He hadn't tinged his words with sarcasm or condemnation but had stated her history as if it were common knowledge.

"I did my duty," she came back at him, defensive, for what she wasn't exactly sure. Men didn't intimidate her. Then why did Mitch? "And I'd do it again. Fighting an enemy I could see was easier than all... this." Her gaze rolled over the windows behind him, the wide executive glass and carved wooden desk, and the lovely carved mermaid in the corner of that desk.

He didn't so much as lift a brow. "You find

duty to family more difficult to accept than duty to country."

"It's not that simple." But yes. As tough as the Army life was, it was simpler. What you saw was what you got. There was no drama. Just structure and teamwork. Goals a determined man or woman could reach. Achievable dreams. Brothers and the occasional sister who had your back.

"Then explain it to me," Mitch said, his clear brown eyes calm and kind. "Help me understand what you find objectionable with your father's work."

Colby looked away, not willing to bare her soul to anyone who worshipped the capitalism that had made Quaid, Incorporated what it was today. It would've helped if Mitch had stuck with that rabid protector of the dynasty routine. But now...

"Let me tell you what you would've seen if you'd accompanied Burton to one of his job sites." His tone dropped to a near whisper. "Burton liked people, Colby. They were always his first priority. I remember his first hare-brained idea: Building single-family dwellings in Rio."

Mitch shook his head, a hint of a smile tweaking the corners of his mouth. "Homes for the homeless, he called it. Yet, to get enough capital to build those houses, he first had to successfully negotiate a contract for an outrageous complex in Dubai. So he did. You've seen the building lauded on the news, I'm sure. It's the only one of its kind in the world, constructed completely of polished steel and high-density polycarbonate."

He leaned forward as if closing the distance between them physically might close the philosophical gap as well. "It's glass, Colby, and it's one of a kind. Burton's end-game was never about being rich or popular, though he achieved both before he died. From day one, it was about using corporate profits to improve the human condition of his fellow mankind. Burton was always about people."

She'd since re-engaged, eyeing Mitch with some measure of disbelief. All of this would've mattered if her father hadn't left his wife and only child behind to help all those other people. Yes, she'd had a life of privilege. Just. Not. Him.

Had he ever come to a single game? Had he ever stood in the stadium at Nickerson Field and cheered when his little girl scored the winning goal despite her sprained ankle, dislocated shoulder, and black eye? No. Burton Quaid was always off saving the world, and Bella Quaid? She was just another casualty of his high ideals, left behind and as needy as Colby.

Mitch had more to say. "I had the privilege of working with one of the greatest humanitarians in the world, and maybe you didn't know, but Burton shunned publicity. He saw it as a hindrance to his mission. He was always so proud of you. I hope at least you know that."

"He was never there," she offered simply. "I didn't travel with him because he never asked me to." How childish she sounded. She would've loved to have gone on any one of those long trips with him. Why hadn't she asked to go? Not even once?

Mitch straightened. "I know you mostly through your father's eyes, Colby, and you're exactly like he was. You expect results, but you want things done your way or the highway. You want to make a difference in the world. You want your life to matter, and you're willing to fight for it. The only difference between him and you is that he knew what he wanted—to help others. I'm not sure you know where you'll be next week much less in ten years."

Karma's a bitch. Wasn't that the same question she'd tossed at Ash just hours ago? *What am I doing in ten years?* Hell, she didn't know what her plan was for the next month. Apparently, there was a lot she didn't know.

"Let me ask an easier question," Mitch said. "Why'd you join the Army?"

That answer she knew. Automatically, her lower jaw slid forward. She rolled her shoulder and tossed her chin at the question. "To stand on my own two feet." *For the first damned time in my life.* "To be known as Colby Quaid, not just as the spoiled brat of Quaid, Incorporated. The rich girl." *To spit in the media's eye and tell all those back-stabbers to fuck off.* "To stand for the right instead of just what corporate greed says is right. To actually do good in the world." *God, I do sound like my dad.* Her fingers curled on her lap, not a good sign.

A genuine smile broke over Mitch's face. "You're Burton reincarnated is who you are, Colby. Full of fire, piss, and vinegar, ready to change the world. Dying to spit at convention and lead the way. That's why you're one of the first female Rangers, isn't it?"

She had a sudden urge to bite her nails. *Maybe...*

It's been a long time since any guy bested her, but damn. What's a person supposed to say when personal revelations just kept coming? She tossed her head, not willing to admit to anything—not yet—but willing to listen a while longer. Maybe she did have what it took to keep Quaid, Incorporated afloat. For that matter, did it even need her? Mitch seemed to have everything handled. Even her...

The cell phone in her hip holster buzzed an incoming. Tula. Probably with another question she'd answer herself. Colby nodded at Mitch as she stood to leave. "Excuse me. I need to take this call."

Before the phone made it to her ear, Tula screeched, "You can get home quick, can'tcha? 'Course you can. Fire, Colby! The house is on fire!"

CHAPTER TWELVE

It was the out of place drift of petrol fumes in the mudroom that caught Ash's attention just as the blast of dragon fire sent him flying. He'd barely stepped outside the back door to dump the trash. When he came to in the small courtyard outside Bella's back porch, shaking his head and wondering *what the hell?* flames already licked up the rear wall of Colby's childhood home. Long streaks of black smoke billowed skyward. *Ah, clapboard paneling. Damn that stuff. It'll burn like the Devil hisself.*

Ash charged up the back steps, cursing his

stupidity for leaving two women inside a burning building. The brass doorknob blistered his right hand, but not once did he consider letting loose of it, not with Bella and Tula in danger. Adding the force of his shoulder to the job, he forced the heavy oak door to yield. The jamb splintered on the second battering, the thing no doubt made of porous pine instead of dense oak, saints be praised. Shoving the door out of his way, Ash choked on his first breath of the oily black smoke coming from the kitchen.

"Tula!" he bellowed, storming past the breakfast nook, where he'd only just been sketching his master plan for a new warehouse. 'Twas a scary heartbreak seeing through the wretched smog between him and the hallway, but he plowed through. Throwing an arm to his forehead to ward off more smoke, he coughed and stumbled on, intent on making it to Bella's room.

"Here! We're here!" Tula screamed from the second story landing with Colby's poor mother on her feet and clinging to Tula's arm.

Finally, a reprieve in the. smoke. The sooty cloud seemed content to stay at the rear of the grand home. Ash waved his way through the last of it and pounded up the curved staircase, watchful for flames and fear in his throat. "Did you call the fire brigade? Nine-one-one?"

"You bet I did," Tula yelled back at him. "Now help me get Miss Bella out of here!"

Ash bent to scoop the older woman off her feet. Still in her nightgown and bed jacket, Bella's arms circled his neck. The poor thing was breathing hard, her eyes wide with fear.

"Are you the one who started this fire?" she asked in a trembling voice.

"No, ma'am," he assured her as he made his way swiftly down the grand staircase. "I would nah do such a despicable thing, nah to anyone. Hold on tight. I don't want to be dropping a lady as fine as you."

By then, sirens screeched outside. The wooden staircase vibrated under the assault of heavy truck engines. Smoke still billowed into the massive entry from the kitchen, but Ash had yet to spy any tongues of flame drawing close to the stairs.

His heart pounded at the awful danger they were in. The smoke was bad enough, but fire was a different kind of sinister beast. It crept inside walls and along two-by-four studs and joists like spiders and snakes did. It slithered, almost as if it were alive, along the many crawl spaces in older homes, winding its way to oxygen and explosive freedom. It purred as it made its nest in unseen pockets of air before it belched through lathe and sheetrock into life. They had to get out of there.

"Are you behind me, Lass?" he called over his shoulder to Tula.

Her hand on his tender neck confirmed her location. "Right behind you, Mister Callahan. Just keep moving, and don't you dare drop my girl."

Her steady touch on his neck felt as if his skin had just slipped, but he didn't care. Relief that Colby had gone into the city flooded him. Quickly, he led his charges to the front entry. Bella twisted in his arms. "Where's my cat? Aren't you going to save him, too?"

"You have a cat?" he nearly shrieked. Was she out of her mind? Why hadn't she mentioned she had a pet until now? He turned on Tula. "Seriously? A cat?" *Please tell me she's wrong, maybe—God forgive me for thinking it—a little looney.*

Tula lifted both shoulders. "I haven't seen that beast in days. I was hoping he'd gotten out and run off."

Ah, damn. It was true then. Ash ducked low and pressed Bella's face under his chin to protect her as they made their dash to freedom. "Suck in a deep breath before you open that door, Tula.

You'll nah be able to breathe if the fire follows us out."

Her eyes went wild, but she nodded and did what he asked.

"You too, Mum," he told Bella. "Take a deep breath and turn your pretty face to me chest. Don't scream no matter what happens. I do nah want to be dropping you."

She nodded, her nose flattened against him as... one... two... three... Tula threw the door open and ran for her life. "Good girl," he muttered, the fire beast not licking at his back as he'd feared.

Two firemen grabbed onto him and Bella at the doorway, manhandling them off the front porch and down to the waiting medics on the walk. It took a full minute to shake the adrenaline off, but by every last one of his Catholic saints, Ash had gotten Colby's family out. Poor Tula stood weeping over the gurney Bella lay on. *Thank God in heaven, they're safe.*

Ash locked his knees to keep from falling to the sidewalk. Blowing out his fear, he sucked in a mighty breath before he backtracked to the fireman at the door. "I've got to be going back in. There's a cat." *A feckin' cat that had better have nine bloody lives.* But he couldn't leave it to burn any more than he'd left Bella and Tula.

"You're not entering that house again," the fireman, a muscular, barrel-chested boy, declared with iron in his voice. "What color? What's its name?"

Bella's face wrinkled in—delight? Was she out of her mind? "He's black," she spit out with a string of drool. "Black with a white goatee under his chin. His name is Pierre. You be nice to him." She pinched her chin as if she needed to make sure they knew where goatees grew.

Ash grabbed hold of the fireman's rubberized sleeve. "I can help you look for it."

"Stay put, sir. If I can find it, I'll be right back. If I can't…" He left those word unsaid as he turned his back on Ash and stomped into the house. Smoke billowed while neighbors gathered on the sidewalk and traffic came to a halt in the now engine filled street.

Am I bad luck? Ash wondered. Two fires in as many days, and he'd been associated with both. Running a quick hand over his face, he waved off the medic approaching him with a small oxygen tank and mask. "I'm fine. See to the women."

"Ash!" That demanding bellow could only be Colby.

Turning, he barely had time to catch her before

she barreled into him. Full force. Her arms snaked around his bloody neck, which for some reason hurt like a bugger. He didn't understand why she was hugging him, but his heart warmed at her reaction. "I'm fine," he muttered, his palms on her butt, holding her to him as tightly as she gripped his neck. He breathed her scent in, letting it restore his balance. She always smelled so good.

"'Tis your mum I'm worried about."

"Where is she?" Colby's fair hair brushed his lips when she spun toward to the medics.

Ash took another deep breath before he released his woman, then went with her to the ambulance where Tula waited with Bella.

There was no cause for alarm. Both women were in good hands, and neither had suffered burns nor smoke inhalation. Still, the medics were thorough, paying extra attention to Bella. Despite the fine weather, they'd wrapped her in heated blankets up to her chin.

Her eyes sparkled at all the young men doting on her as they took her blood pressure and temp, recording everything in their digital tablets. One offered her a hard candy. Her shoulders scrunched as she opened her mouth, and he popped it in. The look on her lovely face caught at Ash's heart. So childlike. So pure. The truth slammed into him then. Her time in this world was very short. He tugged Colby backward and into his arms, frightened that he might be right.

Just then, the brave bloke who'd gone inside to rescue Bella's cat, returned with a squirming, hissing mass of shiny black fur and claws. Another fireman offered an opened cat crate, and in Pierre went, whiskers first, to roam no more. The cat made three that were safe and sound. Ash blew out a bellyful of relief. 'Twas a Hail-Mary-save kind of day after all.

"Your neck. Oh, Ash, crap, you're burned," Colby said, her fingers tracing over the rounded collar of his shirt as she lifted it from his skin.

He flinched her stinging touch away. "Am I now?"

Stretching up on her toes to get a closer look, her pretty lips curved like Cupid's best bow right before she bit them. Could a woman look any more delectable? Any sweeter? Aye. As if she owned the place, Colby turned on a dime into a drill sergeant with attitude. Waving the medics over with a snap of her fingers, she ordered Ash to the curb with a firm, "Stay."

Too bloody tired to remind her that he was not a dog, he folded his long legs and took a seat.

"'Tis a small thing," he insisted to the woman kneeling at his side, fussing over him. Funny, he'd dreamed of a moment like this, but it didn't feel— right. "Let me be, woman. Go take care of your mum. She needs you more right now than I."

Like Colby would ever listen? In no time at all, Ash was bent forward while the two medics worried at his neck. Feeling a draft, he took a better look over his shoulder. They'd cut his shirt without so much as a by your leave. "Is it that bad, then?" he asked, noticing the blood for the first time.

"Yes. The back of your neck's badly burned," Colby explained. "You risked your life to save Mom."

He pinched his itchy nose but took a hard look at her. Colby's amber eyes brimmed with tears. She kept biting her bottom lip. "There now," he lifted a hand to her jaw, not wanting her to cry over the likes of him. "I'm nah hurt that bad. Hardly feel a—ouch, damn it—thing." He glared at the medic who'd just poked him. "You'll nah be doing that again, will ya?"

"Sorry, sir," the young man said. "Could you tilt your head down a little farther, so I can put more of this gel on you? The pain should go away in a minute, but I need to be able to reach the entire burned area."

"Am I really burned that bad?" Huh. Didn't feel a thing until he'd gotten outside.

Colby shook her head, her eyes big and teary, and her blonde hair beautifully ruffled around her face like a halo. "You're incredible," she whispered. "Crazy, but incredible."

CHAPTER THIRTEEN

"The Beantown Stalker? Here?" Colby couldn't believe her ears.

"Do you think he's after me then?" Ash asked even as his left palm settled easily over her right knee, the one closest to his chair. This Irishman had nerve. She chalked his cocky over-confidence up to the wild morning and let it ride.

For now, they sat opposite Fire Chief Kevin Hayden's desk at Boston's Fire Station on Cambridge Street. It was late afternoon on a beautiful spring day. The weather was still cool enough, she'd worn a light windbreaker over a

Navy-blue button up shirt tucked into her favorite stone-washed jeans. After years in the olive drab, she valued a *civilian* wardrobe.

Daylight savings time hadn't rolled the clocks over yet, and the sun was due to set in the west within the hour. Fire chiefs, it seemed, worked around the clock.

"That's the thing," Kevin said, his gray eyes sharp behind his horn-rimmed glasses. "The arson investigator uncovered some very strange things since your place went up in smoke. Mind if I ask who you bought your shipment of Brazilian rosewood from?"

Ash's brows angled upward in surprise. "What are you talking about? I don't import rosewood. 'Tis endangered, man. I could lose me business license if I were daft enough to buy the stuff, nah to mention the fines I'd get." He let out a cocky snicker. "What have you been smoking?"

Kevin's gaze dropped to the unopened file folder on his desk. Pursing his lips, he lifted his gaze to Ash, not a trace of amusement in his eyes. "We've been friends since you came to Boston but mind me now. This is serious. Things will go easier for you if you're straight with me from the get go. We found ebony in our investigation, too.

That wood's just as illegal to buy and import as the rosewood."

"I am being straight with you," Ash answered, his head cocked. "Who found ebony? You? Where? Nah in me shop, you didn't."

Colby leaned forward, her elbows to the edge of the desk. Ash's grip on her knee remained firm and annoying and—warm. Damn near seductive. It was an unwelcome distraction she didn't need in the middle of this investigation, but could she bring herself to brush it off? She thought about it. "You don't really suspect Ash, do you?" she asked. "He's your friend. You've known him for years."

Kevin ran a hand over his red hair as he pushed back in his chair. "I'll be honest with the two of you. No, the ebony and rosewood were not found in your specific shop, Ash, but there've been five fires now." He lifted three fingers. "At the first three, we found burned and scorched pallets of lumber, some logs, and other wood-related products in the debris. It's taken our investigator this long to put the pieces together and to run down the few leads that didn't burn, but every last one of those rosewood and ebony shipments leads back to you."

He shook his head as if trying to make sense of it. "The investigator also found bills-of-lading listing you as sole receiver, Ash. He's searched the original orders. He's talked to the suppliers, some of them no good, underhanded smugglers. Granted, not all his sources are reputable, but he's located three written orders for those endangered woods, all signed by your hand. If you're dealing with black marketeers, tell me now. We've got you dead to rights, man. Where in my city are you meeting these smugglers?"

Ash grunted, his demeanor surprisingly as steady as his grip on Colby's knee. That thumb of his burned very deliberate circles into the denim. Here, at what could be the end of his reputation and the beginning of a prison sentence, he seemed as cool as if he were simply down at the local pub, ready to throw one back with his drinking buddy. "You know me better than that, Kev. Give me a tablet and a pen if you've got one handy. I'll give you me written name to compare with your supposed evidence."

Kevin couldn't look Ash in the eye, and he blinked rapidly, as if conflicted—or his eyes were extremely dry. After a minute or so, he dug a paper tablet out of his side drawer and tossed it with a pen to Ash, though how Ash meant to sign it one-handed remained to be seen. His steady attention to Colby's knee was slowly working her last nerve—her starving, *I-haven't-had-sex-in-years* last nerve. The smallest sizzle crept along the inseam of her jeans like a flame, reaching higher. Still, she did nothing to discourage him.

"I can't show you the evidence," Kevin admitted, "but I'd be pleased if you'd give me several samples of your writing. I've got nothing else to fight this case they're building against you."

Ah, so he did intend to fight it. Good to know. Colby leaned her elbows to the desk, while Ash maintained his hold on her knee while he adeptly stroked off several signatures with his right hand.

"Who's building a case, Kevin?" Why did her voice sound breathy? Colby cleared her throat and asked more evenly, "Are we looking at one arson investigator or several?"

"That's where I have my greatest misgivings." Kevin's gaze flickered to Ash. "Well, my second greatest. I'm sorry, Ash. This is as hard on me as it is you. Truth be known, this coincidence raised considerable flags in our investigation. Leviathan Mutual is the underwriter behind the first three arsons. They're the ones building this case against you."

"Interesting," Colby said as she cocked her

head, not believing what she'd heard. It was getting harder to focus. That simmering trail of sparks had morphed into yearning. Why couldn't Ash keep his hands to himself?

Kevin nodded. "That's not all. They've got a bulldog of an insurance investigator who knows a lot about you. He's laying for you, Ash. I'm surprised he hasn't caught up with you yet. The last time I had the unpleasant duty to meet with him, he had some very unkind things to say about you."

Ash didn't rise to the bait and ask what those things were like Colby would've. He kept his cool, as if this were just a misunderstanding amongst friends over a game of pool. "I've nah been home," he admitted as he handed the tablet back to Kevin, his left fingers still very much in play. "There you go. Check those against your evidence."

Nodding, Kevin flipped his file folder open, tracking the signatures on his sheets of evidence against Ash's. The poor man's forehead glistened, and he licked his lips as down the pages he went.

Colby threaded her right hand through the stray tendrils at her temple. She wouldn't want to be in Kevin's shoes, having to question the integrity of his friend. He and Ash went back ten years that she knew of. Unlike Hammer, he was the steady wingman who'd showed at every soccer match alongside Ash. Sometimes, in face paint. Sometimes with hand painted signs boasting of her wicked killer instincts on the field. She licked her bottom lip and wished for a breath of cool, fresh air. Or a stiff drink. *Is it hot in here?*

At last, Kevin lifted his face to the ceiling. His cheeks ballooned and his chest swelled with a deep breath. "Oh, for the love of Mike, you're a life saver, Ash. Not a one of these signatures is a match to the bills of lading. They're not even close, and I'm proud to know you. Thank the Lord for small favors."

"And large ones in return," Colby breathed, though where that sentiment had sprung from, she had no idea. It just blurted out of her.

Ash leaned his elbow to the edge of the desk, his chin resting on the heel of his free hand. "Of course, they don't, Kev. I didn't write them. You had to know that."

Kevin nodded, wiping his brow with the back of his hand. With another deep breath, he smiled for the first time since he'd sat down. "I did, brother, I truly did. 'Tis a madman we're up against. If he's targeting you, no one you care about will be safe. I'm calling the police to put all of you in protective custody."

"Nah." Ash waved him off as he reclined into his seat again, a true study in self-control. "I'll nah be bullied by the likes of a sneaky coward with a can of petrol and a match. Let him come at me again, and I'll bust his balls. Would you like me to carve off one for a souvenir for you?"

Kevin's ruddy face beamed. "I would at that, but I can't let you take the chance." When Ash huffed his annoyance, Kevin brushed it off with, "At least let me move Colby and her mother out of town 'til this is settled. Then maybe you and I will run this bugger to ground and be done with him."

"Uh-uh, I'm not going anywhere," Colby shot back at him. For all his good intentions, that would be the day she ran and hid while the men folk did the dirty work. She was trained for this.

It took her a full minute to realize Ash was grinning at her, not until Kevin chin nodded to him and said, "You're right. I can see it. Best to keep on her good side, boyo." To Colby he said, "Are you certain you're not related to Grace Malone?"

"Who?" She had to ask.

Ash's hand moved from her knee to cup her elbow. "Never mind, love. I'll explain, but first I have something to show you. Later, Kev. If you need another one of me autographs, just ask." Sticking his thumb to the end of his nose, he wiggled his fingers. "I can do this all day."

Kevin reached across the desk and snagged Ash's hand in one of those guy grips that went up to each other's elbows. "Keep an eye out. This bloke could've killed you and everyone in that house today. By the by, you haven't seen Hammer lately?"

"I did. We threw a few back last night, least 'til his phone rang and he had to run. The man's whipped, Kev. Like a good little boy, one call is all it takes, and off he goes to his wife."

Kevin's head bobbed knowingly. "Aye, I've noticed it, too. His poor missus seems to be sick a lot."

"I'm nah sure of what though. Hammer never talks about her, just ups and takes off when she rings," Ash said as he snaked a hand around her waist and tugged Colby to her feet.

Ordinarily, she would've given him a proper shove off, but not today. There was something about the rugged strength of the guy who'd saved her mother's life. Ash had displayed uncommon valor. For the first time in a long while, she leaned into a man for more than just another pack of ammo.

"It'd be best if you two stayed out of sight until we've got this bloke behind bars," Kevin said.

"Or dead," Colby added. "If he comes after my mom again, I'll end him."

Kevin nodded at her in that patronizing, yeah-right way of so many men. But Ash was the smart one. He leaned into her cheek, whispering, "And I'll be there to help you bury the body, love."

She could've kissed him right there and then, but Kevin's chair screeched when he pushed back. He stood and waved them off. "Stop it, you two! I can't hear another word. My ears are slammed tight."

"Sláinte," Ash said easily as he pulled Colby to her feet.

Kevin mellowed, a friendlier smile on his face. "And to you. May you both be well and smiling. Now be gone with you!"

Chapter Fourteen

Once outside the fire station, Ash took a deep breath of springtime. Poor Kev was in a bad spot. All of those arson-caused fires had occurred inside his jurisdiction. The press was eating him and the department's arson investigators for breakfast, lunch, and dinner.

'Twas a tough job putting out fires around the clock, then having to confront his buddy for the heinous crime of burning another's property, endangering life and limb. So far, no one had died, but the fates were gradually realigning the stars in the universe. It was only a matter of time before an innocent was caught in the line of fire.

Ash kept his hand at Colby's waist, surprised she hadn't elbowed him or told him to knock it off yet. She turned at the car door he'd just opened for her. "Where are we going? And since when did you own a Lexus?"

A different light glowed in her eyes tonight, and it sparkled at him as she sank into the seat. He winked and shut the door in her face. Strolling around the rear of the vehicle, he tossed the Lexus' key fob into the air just because. The vehicle wasn't his, but there'd come a time, maybe sooner than later, that he'd drive a car just as fine. But if he never did, well, he'd be just as good as he was right now, wouldn't he? Because now—Ash knew.

It'd been a long day, but with Bella and Tula moved to a fancy five-star hotel in town, he felt reborn. His warehouse burning had dealt him a blow he'd not seen coming, but the fire at Bella's home on Beacon Hill did something just as unexpected. As the day wore on, he'd come to realize what her mother's death would've done to Colby. He'd seen the devastation in her eyes out there on the street when she'd run to her mum. She'd been a scared little girl in those few seconds it took her to get to Bella, her tears running unabashedly down her cheeks.

Ash couldn't get the look of blessed relief on her pretty face when she'd caught up with her mum, out of his mind. Colby was a puzzle to him, a mix of muscle and grit over a heart as big as the Atlantic. He had to wonder at the hardness to her, if it wasn't more a shell game she played, and if it wasn't mostly herself she was fooling. Normally outspoken, brash and bold, he'd seen a different side to Colby today. She'd reminded him of a fragile rose that could've easily been crushed had the morning gone badly.

Snapping the fob out of the air, he opened his car door, feeling worthy for the first time in— forever. Because Ash Callahan, the ne-er-do-well, had been reborn, baptized, and confirmed with that one lightning bolt of scorching revelation. It was nothing less than an epiphany, one he should've seen coming. He'd read the good book often enough to know it was true. Sweet Mother Mary and Joseph, he'd been an altar boy for Christ's sake. Some days he wondered how hard his skull really was. The truth had finally sunk in. Sinners could change. They could repent and be forgiven, and drunkards could be reformed. Even he.

Folding his angular frame into the Lexus, Ash joined Colby in the plush confines of modern technology, soft lighting, and that new car smell. He hit the ignition, then turned his eyes on the one true good thing in his life.

He knew it now. His success as a man was not defined by his livelihood or his ambition. Neither was it was not found in the passion in his soul, the one he let loose with his hands when he pulled mermaids and beautiful women out of wood. Nah. His success, his one true dream was Colby.

For years he had thought he had to change, that he had to be strong enough or rich enough. Man enough. But now he knew. He could nah change the passion in his heart for the love of this fierce woman. He was, by all the saints, good enough just the way he was.

She still smiled, her shoulders angled toward him. "Okay, give. You've had a smug smile on your face since you picked me up at the hotel. Where'd you get this car?"

Ah, so the expensive car impressed her. He shrugged off his annoyance at that discomfiting discovery. But a woman born into luxury would notice a fine automobile. "It's not mine. Hammer loaned it to me for the duration."

She pinched her lips into a pout, one he wanted to run his thumb over. Or bite. But not yet. "Where are we going? Where's this thing you want to show me?"

He hummed. He hawed. Then he decided to stick with his plan. Checking the rearview, h pulled into traffic. "You'll see."

The best sound a man can hear? His woman's sigh of contentment. When Colby leaned back into the buttery softness of good leather with a sigh, that simple exhalation whispered up Ash's spine like the lazy finger of forever. He just hoped she'd be as content with him as the Lexus.

Tonight had the potential of being one of those rare moments in a man's life when whatever happened next would either make him or break him. It all depended on Colby.

The vehicle handled smoothly to the right past the New England Aquarium, and across the bridge to his flat. He wanted her to see what he'd kept for himself, the single masterpiece that had escaped the flames because he'd been too selfish to share it, much less sell it. He might yet have to, if that insistent bloke from Cape Cod didn't stop calling, wanting what he'd ordered. But Ash could carve another. He could. It might not be precisely the same, but aye. He'd do what he had to do for Colby.

Once off Seaport Boulevard, he jockeyed past road construction and the dark waters of the Reserve Channel at his left, to First Street. Just blocks to the east, his woodworking shop lay in smoldering ruins and charred timbers with police tape fluttering the perimeter, warning looters and mischief-makers to keep back.

But did that burned husk of his old dreams matter in the grand scheme of this new day? Not anymore. Ash pulled alongside his flat, the second door on the right in a complex of sturdy, well-worn row houses. Before Colby could comment on stopping at what she knew was his place, he scrambled to open her door.

"Why are we here?" He could've kissed that stern raised brow of hers.

"'Tis not what you think." *But it could be.* He placed one hand at the small of her back and urged her forward with his other.

They climbed the twelve steps to number eighteen-fifty-three, First Street. He unlocked the deadbolt, and for the first time in his American existence, he'd brought a girl home. Maybe not home to Mum and Da, but still. This was one of *those* moments.

Flipping the light switch just inside the door, he welcomed Colby into his dingy little corner of the United States. Okay, so now he was wishing he'd put a little more forethought into this ruse and done a bit of proper housekeeping. But honestly. What'd she expect from a man, Martha Stewart-type decor? His clothes hung up in proper order in some unseen closet? Maybe a sprig of lilacs on his table instead of books and tools and the groceries he had yet to store? Not happening.

Ignoring Colby's confusion, he steered her, wordlessly, into his small living room, past the tiny kitchen at his right, and to the bedroom opposite his at the end of the narrow hall. Her feet dragged more with each step, her body growing more resistant, but she needed to see this. Once and for all, she needed to know what she meant to him.

With his heart beating as loud as the thunderous bass drums in Saint Paddy's Day parade, he reached around Colby and opened the door. Another light switch and another gasp of what he hoped was surprise-and-awe instead of shock-and-damn-you-to-hell.

He swallowed hard, his mouth dry and in desperate need of a gulp of creamy, cold Guinness now that his soul was on the chopping block.

Step by step, she ventured though the door of the crowded second bedroom turned woodworking shop. "W-what...?"

Aye, he knew she'd be speechless when she saw it. So the bloody hell was he.

Colby cocked her head, first to one side, then the other, as if she couldn't believe what she was seeing. "H-how...?"

The poor thing was as flummoxed at the sight of his creation as he often was looking at her.

Ash held his breath, needing her to spit out whatever it was she was feeling. For all his thirty years, watching her still made him as giddy as a schoolboy. Did she like it? Would she be angry? Would she think he'd violated her in a creepy, stalker kind of way? Gods in heaven, he couldn't think with his blood thrumming hot and volatile through his body like it was. Sweat beaded at his temple as Ash licked his lips. Maybe this was nah such a good idea after all. Was he daft thinking this would ever—?

But it was too late to stop the thing he'd set in motion. Colby was now in the room, her head still cocked as she took in the only treasure that had not burned to its death yesterday morn. Her voice was as quiet as the dust motes hanging in the light over her pretty head. "It's... it's me?"

CHAPTER FIFTEEN

"Nah," he said, his voice a gentle grate against her sensitive eardrums. "'Tis not you. Miss Colby Quaid, meet Her Highness, Grace O'Malley, the Queen of Umaill, the fearless chieftainess of the mighty O'Maill clan, and the seafaring scourge of the British crown." He bowed. Ash actually bowed like a gentleman to the wooden statue.

"The Irish pirate?" She had to ask. "Was this what Kevin meant?" *Or who.*

"Aye, the fighting O'Malleys of Rockfleet Castle."

Colby couldn't believe her eyes. This wasn't some legendary Irish female pirate. *Uh-uh.* There, in the center of Ash's cramped little spare bedroom, as tall as the ceiling and resting in an equally large wooden cradle, surrounded by a pool of wooden curlicues and shavings and sawdust was—her. Colby Quaid. In the very naked flesh. Every exposed peak and crevice of her.

An orderly row of woodcarving tools: gouges, chisels, blades, and mallets, rested on the canvas covered table against the wall to her right, but she couldn't not look at the giant carved wooden statue of—*oh my. It's... it's me.*

It was one of those magnificent creations that hung from the prows of masted schooners of old. Of pirate ships. The lady's bare feet and legs wept behind her, her ankles crossed as if she'd risen from the waves. Her head was up and her chin lifted as if into a stiff wind. Her eyes were carved of clear amber, the pupils big and black.

As if she wasn't already enough of a magical apparition, the wooden queen held a crystal blue globe in her raised palms aloft, as if offering a tithe to Neptune—or some nautical god of Ash's very fertile imagination. Interestingly, a feathery tendril of ivy twined between her full breasts to circle her waist before it dipped to her sex, intimately covering that one part of her bare body.

My body. Bared. What was it Ash always said? Jesus, Mary, and Joseph? Yeah. That.

Colby swallowed hard, every step around this piece of art, an insight into the romance and skill of the man in the room. He hadn't said a word since he'd opened the door to this startling revelation. This secret.

Meeting Grace Malone in the flesh certainly wasn't what she'd expected when he'd pulled up to the curb. The man was a player. A panty melting, drop dead gorgeous male, who whether he knew it or not, pulled wanton glances from women he passed on the street. She'd anticipated a drink and the promise of a tussle—if he was lucky. But this...

Wow. Her heart pounded as hard and as fast as it often had before battle. There were no words. Suddenly weak in the knees, she rested one palm to the curvy hip of this fantastical replica of—*me. Wow. I can't believe it's...My God. It's me.*

While most of the creation had been carved from a rich, honey gold wood, the mounds of billowing hair around the pirate queen's face held a decidedly reddish tint, nearly the same as her natural hair color before the desert suns of the Mideast had bleached the life out of it—and her.

Streaks of darker red ran alongside streams of pure gold. Carved curls, spirals, and tangles dripped in a mass down the statue's back that led to a sumptuous ass. Even if Colby thought that fabulous figure was the true image of herself, she'd never tell Ash. Not him, the eternal rogue who fancied himself a lady's man, considered his future wife nothing more than domestic staff. Many men married simply to replace their mothers or because they needed a slave, someone foolish enough to cook, clean, and cater to their every whim. *But that person is not me.*

But this woman... this figurehead. Something else again. What on earth was he trying to tell her?

"You like strawberry blondes," she whispered past the dry catch in her throat. *And apparently, very naked women.*

"Aye." He covered a cough. "But just one."

Another revelation, one she'd known for years but hadn't had the guts to face. The player it seemed was not what she'd thought he was, but then. Was she? "This must've taken a while to carve." *Like years.*

Another, "Aye," and footsteps rustled over the sawdust on the floor as warm hands descended to her shoulders. Was he as nervous as she was? "This is me first." His voice had turned decidedly raspy. Hoarse, as if his throat was dry and he needed a drink. She certainly did. "I made another down at me warehouse. Some rich bloke up in Cape Cod ordered it, but that one burned."

Of course, the creation was nude. This was Ash, after all. But as he would say, "Bloody hell," Colby breathed, her sharp eyes still taking in details only a close friend—or a lover—would've known. Like the tiny scar at the corner of her left eye where she'd been gouged by some asshat's fingernail in a hard-won soccer game against Quincy, Mass. That was one for the records, more of a catfight than competition.

But he'd also caught the very full breasts Colby had once wrapped and bound before games to keep them out of her way. As a driven athlete, she'd had no use for that much jiggle, had even considered a surgical reduction. But now?

She ran her fingers over the wooden peak of a perfect nipple, smiling at that devilish mind behind her. Sliding her fingertips down the carved lady's ribcage, she spied a mole above the left hip identical to hers. Colby pinched her lips, fighting a chuckle. Though he'd never seen her naked, Ash still knew her body well. Even the hollow of her butt cheeks, the dimple where those cheeks flared. The embarrassing size of them.

Wow. Does this little room make my butt look big? Heat lapped at her cheeks and prickled up her neck. *Oh, my, my, my...* Colby stifled the girly impulse to fan herself at the knowledge that he'd had his hand on her ass, by proxy maybe, but still. This was definitely her butt.

The tiny room was suddenly unspeakably warm. He knew her body better than she knew his. Her only glimpse of him in the buff had been this morning, and yes, the glorious sight had nearly done her in.

At last, the master cleared his throat. "This is the original. Like I said before, I made another for a customer, but it burned in the fire. I could nah sell this one, nah for all the gold nor silver in the land. If you do nah like it, I—"

She whirled on him, still fighting the smile tugging at her lips. "It's...." *So hard to describe.* "...the most..." *Still working here.* "...interesting woman I've ever seen," she offered, the warmest parts of her body throbbing. Her belly clenched. Other places, too.

A shadow shifted in those glorious blues of the rowdy male standing before her. "Interesting?"

he repeated as if the word soured on his tongue.

Colby grinned. Giggled. Bit her lip, then stuck her chin at him. "It's me, Ash. I can't very well say she's the most stunning woman I've ever seen when she's me, can I?"

"Aye, 'tis you." There it was, the smile she hadn't realized she'd been waiting for. It blossomed over Ash's rugged face like the morning sun over the Hindu Kush in springtime. In two steps, she was in his arms. He spun her in a slow circle, his hand cupping the back of her head, while she carefully held onto his biceps since his poor neck was off limits. "It took me a year to carve her," he said earnestly. "Another to get her perfect, then another to sand and polish. Another to protect..."

Colby's heart stalled. *Protect.* He'd been working on this masterpiece, imbuing it with his protection, since she'd joined the Army? Why does one man do something like this for the woman who'd left him behind? What a waste of time! Why had he obsessed and poured his heart into a silly piece of wood just because...?

Oh, my God, He loves me. Ash Callahan really loves me.

"You've had your hands on me for years." She made that a quiet observation, fighting the noisy beat of her heart. *He truly loves me.*

Ash nodded. "And in me heart, Lass. With every nick and gouge, every careful pare, cut and sweep, I said a Hail Mary for you. Just for you. I prayed to the Holy Virgin you'd come home safe and well, and I..." His eyes turned dark and black as his pupils expanded, drawing her in. "Even if you didn't return to me, I begged the Lord to please let you live through your trials, Colby. To at least keep you safe, so you could do whatever it is you want with your life. Just to bring you home, Lass. That's all I asked the good Lord for. You coming back alive was enough for me."

He hadn't said: Bring you home *to me.* Just *bring you home.* The ultimate sacrifice of true love. *Simply to let me go and let me live...*

Her heart swelled. This man, this reckless, romantic, aggravating male with eyes as blue as the deep blue sea might not be the player she'd thought he was. Like her mother and her father, like Quaid, Inc., she might've completely missed the mark. Ash was more than the cheeky Irishman she'd judged him to be.

Lifting her hands to his shoulders, she aligned her thumbs with his collarbones, and her breasts with his broad chest. The man's arms and body surrounded her with adoration, just like his sacrifice. "So tell me about Grace O'Malley." *If you can...*

CHAPTER SIXTEEN

One thing led to another. Ash meant to speak of history and the fine oaken carving in his wee flat, he truly did. But somewhere between the proud pirate queen's rousting the British from their siege at Rockfleet in 1574, and her capture by Sir Richard Bingham a few years later, when England, with its land grabbing appetite, outlawed the Irish chieftains, Ash lost what was left of his heart to the magnificent golden lioness at his side.

They'd settled on his couch—not on his bed, mind you, but on his couch as was proper. Well, at least, more proper than taking her straightway to his bed. With every word, the story of the Irish Queen's plundering ways sparked a fire deep in Colby's eyes. When the amber in her irises turned to molten copper, and the black of her pupils swallowed the gleam off the copper, he couldn't catch his breath, nor his balance. With all of his heart and every last breath of his searching, wishing Irish heart, Ash fell.

Down he went, lock, stock, and barrel into the woman behind all his dreams.

Colby wrapped her arms around his head like two steel bands he didn't plan to break even as he maneuvered her head to what had to be the loneliest couch cushion in the world. Saints be praised, it had finally served its intended purpose.

Ash cupped her sweet face between his big rugged palms, his body on fire as he took the time to control himself long enough to peer into her eyes. It wasn't copper he saw there, but the sultry come-on of the woman he'd lost his heart to years ago.

Her chin tilted up in a gesture of defiance. Maybe a dare?

Caught like she was in his callused hands, he meant to go slow, but her skin felt as soft as a lamb's wool and as smooth as satin. Reverently, he lowered his mouth to hers, careful to not frighten her off. Just as careful not to break eye contact. He hadn't the experience of other men, not with women. With whiskey and rum, with smokes and a quick limerick, yes, but never with a real woman. Blame that on his mum.

Sighing, Ash dipped his lips to Colby's, just for a taste. One incredibly succulent taste of... *Ah. Heaven. 'Tis heaven I'm in.*

That single contact took on a life of its own, demanding more. Lighting a flash fire that roared to life under his skin and fought for control of the desire tumbling through his veins. He had no idea how one moment his hands were on her face, the next roving over her shirt, wanting to tear it away, to lay her full breasts as bare as his carved Irish queen's.

Colby shifted her hips, arching up against and bumping his aching manhood, but he dared not break contact with her mouth, not and forgo the moist warm tongue-lashing she was giving him. *Well, blimey. So this is what Colby likes. A steady assault. I can do this.*

He slid one hand to her cheek, then to the hollow of her neck, hoping she'd meant that bump. But if she really wanted this with him, she'd have to lose those clothes of hers on her own. He would nah take what she would not offer.

The minx bit down on his lower lip, enough to amp up his courage and take the chance. The fire in his belly burned as hot as ever. Roses, wind, and gunpowder, that's what he smelled on her, and right now, it was the sweetest ambrosia. A fireball streaked up his spine and he bowed his body into the cradle of her womanly hips, needing release and her forgiveness, and—dare he think it—her love?

Was it in any way possible for the two of them? *Mother Mary and Joseph, I hope so.*

One warm womanly hand drifted from his shoulder to his ribs, then to his ticklish hip. He flinched, not from pain, but that she'd remembered that about him.

Colby gripped harder, her fingernails digging into his skin as she whispered into his open mouth, "I can't do this."

'Don't say it! Nah again!' his heart cried even as Ash thrust against her tongue as vigorously as he could, desperate to change her mind. *'Please give me a chance to prove meself. I am man enough for you. I know I am. Give me—give us—a go.'*

She turned her head, smearing his kiss across her cheek. "Ash. Get off. Let me up."

Her palm was on his chest again. Like last time. They'd never gotten this far. So close. *Shite. Here we go again.*

Ash sat back on his haunches, his manhood deflating in front of her. *Let her look.* Once again, she'd brought him low. Why not let her see him at his worst? He didn't try to hide the shrinking flashlight in his pants. What was the bloody sense in pretending her continual rebuffs didn't hurt?

The second she sat up, she leaned forward, her blonde hair brushing over his forearms and... *Whoosh!* Her t-shirt flew off and over her pretty head.

Ash's entire body sprang back to attention. Did he stand a prayer's chance in hell of making love to this woman? Here? Tonight?

Colby's palms hit his chest again, her fingers splayed wide. She cocked her head with a come-hither sparkle in those sensuous maple syrup eyes. "Ash, come on. Help me out of these jeans."

There was no use fighting the chemistry between them. Colby tossed every last logical argument why this would never work to the street. She'd needed Ash in her life since the day she'd left Boston in her rearview, and she needed him now.

He'd changed, and that change was rough and callused and steadily working its way up her bare thighs, now that her pants were—somewhere out there. Strong fingers carved over her hips and ribs, mapping her flesh, bringing her to life the same as he'd done with that log-turned-pirate-ess in his guest room. Wherever his fingers trailed, molten lava trickled beneath her skin, scorching her in its wake.

As those same bold fingers slid under the elastic of her silk panties, he mashed his mouth to hers, forming a suction that gave her a heady rush of *I've-got-to-have-this-man-inside-me*. Now!

Breathing each other's air, she suckled at his tongue and lips, on fire for the first time in a sweaty exercise that didn't involve balls or guns. At least not soccer balls.

He'd long since tossed his shirt and lost his pants. Ash's body was rough and rugged, the coarse hairs on his chest brushing over her sensitive nipples, peaking them into wanton beggars that waited impatiently for attention from his skillful fingertips. He seemed intent on pouring his heart into his kisses, and she let him. Stubble sanded her chin and lips, but this was what she'd wanted from that first kiss that she hadn't gotten, a roiling volcano primed to erupt at her touch.

Groaning, he licked her lips before his open mouth slathered warm desire over her chin. He bumped her head up with his nose to make room for a warm, wet kiss on her throat. A woman can dream, and during those dark nights in the Mideast and South America, on deployments and risky missions, this was the man she'd dreamed of. Every single time.

His skillful adoration of her body sent shivers coursing over her belly at the prospect of what he had in store for her. At last his hand drifted to her breast, thank God! Colby arched her back, pushing one throbbing mound into his palm.

A manly chuckle of satisfaction sounded. "Tell me what you want," he breathed into the sweaty flesh between her breasts as he cupped both, his thumbs strumming her nipples.

"All of you," she grated, her voice as wanton as she'd never heard it before. With that urgent command, a spark lit the hidden det cord that led to her core. A pool of slick moisture unleashed between her legs.

"'Tis about time," he said, just as his lips drew

her peaked nipple into the moist heat of his fiery mouth.

Ahh, yes! This! Colby shoved herself into him, and in return, he suckled, pulling fire through her quivering body, which was already glowing and awash with scorching flames. Her core wept for him, but that mouth of his wasn't done with her. Those scraping, nipping teeth. The pleasant abrasion of his whiskered chin against her tenderest skin was enough to make her...

"I'm coming," she ground out, her body soaring to heights she'd never imagined or known. "Ash! God, Ash!" *What. A. Rrrrrrrrush!*

Fireworks erupted through Colby like bottle rockets gone wild. Stars! Okay, yes, an unexpected rainbow. It probably had a pot of gold at the end of it, too. She sucked in a breath even as she bit her lip at the height he'd pushed her to. Flying. She was flying and his fingers and lips were the high-octane fueling her ride into...

Heaven! Streaks of sizzling pleasure shivered over her skin and in her veins like champagne bubbles. Colby shuddered as her body clamped onto the hollow space he'd now so perfectly filled. Instinctively, her legs wrapped around him in a desperate crush of needing every last inch of him. He wanted a pirate? How about a starved-for-love

Ranger?

With a grunt of breathless domination, Colby bucked Ash off of her hips and onto his back. "Your turn."

CHAPTER SEVENTEEN

Ash couldn't have been happier at the change in position. Manly satisfaction the likes he'd never known before had washed over him at Colby's passion when she'd screamed his name. From the moment he'd set eyes on her, he'd wanted to bed this lass, but with every beat of his wayward Irish heart now, his soul cried out, 'She loves me! She truly loves me.' And wasn't that every man's dream come true? That an angel so fine as herself would deign to love a weak mortal man as hisself. Aye.

Amber eyes gazed down on him from within

the dripping golden spirals of her honey-blonde hair. Tiger eyes, unblinking and predatory, she was hungry for him. He couldn't've looked away from this beautiful creature for all the gold at the end of the rainbow.

Her lovely chin toss told Ash she'd do as she pleased, and he'd let her. Yet as easily as she'd detonated before, he wondered at her experience with men. With coming. She seemed to know some of what happened between a man and his woman, yet she hadn't touched him yet. Not where it counted.

His nostrils flared, drawing in the rich, sultry scent of her blooming. They'd *discussed* a woman's proper place in the world once before, and it hadn't gone well. She knew how strongly he felt about providing for his woman and being the man of his house, and now was not the time to poke that hornet's nest. Not when he was so close to paradise. Like it or not, she was on top. His hands settled to the flare of her hips and let her lead.

Yet he wanted to know—for certain—just how many, or if any, men she'd known in her Army life.

"You like being on top, do you nah?"

"I think so, yeah." A genuine smile curved her luscious lips, and gah! His staff throbbed to delve as deep as possible into the tender folds of her exquisite body. Even now, he could feel the heat dripping off of her as she opened wider for him.

"There's something you need to know," she murmured as she crushed her breasts to his chest, her hair in his face and her lips in his ear.

He waited, needing her to say the words. There was so much lost little girl in this tough woman, it squeezed the salty tears right out of his eyes. "Yes?" he encouraged gruffly. "I'm listening." *And if it's too hard a thing to speak, I'll gladly wait 'til the day it isn't.*

"I..." Her body tensed from her toes to her lovely lips. A breathy murmur eased out of her with, "You need to know that I've... never done this before, Ash. Gone this far. Needed anyone so much."

A glorious wave of male pride boomed through the rafters of his soul. "You're safe now," he felt the need to tell her, less he crow like he very much felt like doing. "And remember that it's me you're talking to, love. You know I'll never hurt you." Yet he ached so bad from the years of abstinence waiting for her, he could blow his chance before he got properly seated. Just her breath on his ear stretched his endurance, but this precious gift of her purity... This wicked roaring lust in his ears as she slipped one slender hand between them to take hold of him... The mighty need to thrust into her when she shifted her tender body over him...

Gritting his teeth, Ash determined to hold his needs back and go slow if it was the last thing he did. This moment was for her, not him. He wouldn't out maneuver her with his experience or skill of the subject at hand. His knees quaked with restraint even as his soul burst with the sublime knowledge that he was her first.

"Is there something you need or want me to—?" he started to ask when—

Bloody hell! She dropped onto him—impaled herself—in one slick rush. Quick and fast and—gah! So blessedly good his eyes rolled back in his head.

But what was dear, wee lass thinking? Fighting for composure and needing very much to see the expression on her face, Ash cupped her jaws in both hands. Tears? No! "Did I hurt you?"

A nod. Colby bit her bottom lip, not making eye contact. "Did I hurt you?" she had the nerve to ask him in a tight, breathy voice, her lashes lowered as her hips froze in place.

Ah, no, no, no! This was not how her first time should've been. "You cannah hurt me, love, but look at me. Come on, please, don't hide those pretty eyes," he begged, pressing the end of his nose to hers. "Nah anymore. Nah about this."

Swallowing hard, she lifted her lashes now bedecked with crystal tears that she quickly dashed away.

"You should nah have done that so fast," he whispered tenderly, threading his fingers through her hair as he stared into her feminine amber depths. "I'm not bragging, but I'm not exactly a small man, and this is your first time, and I'm humbled beyond the stars that you waited for me. You did wait for me, did you nah?" he asked, daring to hope he was the recipient of a gift so rare. Not that her being a virgin mattered, because he certainly had sown his share of wild oats, but this precious gift counted in ways he'd never imagined. Until now. Until he held her quivering, naked body in his hands, he'd never considered what virginity meant.

He, Ash Callahan, was her first. She'd never shared her body before, yet of all the men she'd surely brushed up against in boot camp and combat, in school and in life, she'd held out for him. It brought a fresh watering of tears to his eyes, was what it did. He'd never deserve her, not in a million years. Shame for being the randy boy he'd been, scalded him now. But there was nothing Ash could do but hold her, and promise to love her without end, and count hisself the absolute luckiest man alive.

"Set for a minute, Colby. Please. Take your time. Get used to it. Get used to me," he said as he smoothed his palms over her shoulder blades, holding her in place lest she think she was up for a rowdy first ride.

She nodded, panting, her palms on his chest, and a sheen of sweat on her brow. "Sorry 'bout that. I wanted to do it right. Guess I didn't think it would h-h-hurt so much... there."

Ah, she was killing him. Not in a million years would he have guessed her extreme need to dominate the field, even now. "You've nothing to be sorry about. Just breathe. In and out. Relax, love." If there were any way to comfort her without stealing her power, he'd carry her to his tub right this very minute. A nice hot bath would soothe her poor self and—

Gah! With another thrust, she'd speared him to the hilt, so tight and so blessedly deep that he was the one who lost eye contact now. Sweet Baby Jesus. The heavenly fit. The friction. In every way, shape, and form, this woman was made for him. But what was going on in that head of hers?

"Bloody hell," he hissed. What she'd just done had to have hurt, but even as that concern materialized, the primal caveman in his soul roared to chest thumping life, and he was caught in a sizzling baptism of virginal fire. Hers. A delectable heatwave tightened his balls and lit his fuse. Fastening her hips to him with his fingertips, he meant to never let her go. She must've understood as slowly, she rolled her hips as if stirring him deep inside her body. Finding her way from his groin to his heart and...

"I'm afraid this is going to be fast," he bit out, his toes curling like a woman's for the gods' sake! How odd? How weird? How feckin'—*ffffffine.*

He thrust upward, filling her, unable to stifle a roar as she rocked. "Colby! Ah, Colby!" He came so fast that he saw stars; red, white and blue instead of the green, white, and orange, not what he'd expected, but so be it. His manhood was tucked finally good and proper inside his All-American girl. Colby had brought him—finally, blessedly—all the way home.

Her being on top definitely had its merits.

Jesus, Mary, and Joseph, he was flying so high, he didn't want to come down. This intimate moment together was worth the pain of the wasted years spent waiting for her. And hoping. Ash held Colby to him in a crushing circle of the purest adoration, from his hands to her hips, his lips to her lips. Did she know how much he loved her? He meant to be sure she did, if only he could speak the words of his heart as easily as she'd just made him—*come.*

He opened his eyes to her knowing smile, but it was bloody hard to see through the misty blur. When he blinked enough to clear the haze, she gave him that chin nod again, her tough girl persona back in full force. "Want more, big boy?"

"Did they teach you that in Ranger school?" he teased, his hands on her shoulders but his breath so hoarse, he wasn't sure she'd heard him.

Colby trailed her index finger up to his navel, where she bent to place a kiss as she whispered, "I'm an all or nothing kind of girl, Ash. Once I make a decision, I don't hold back. I give my all, and I'm in all the way." Her muscles clenched around him, making him gasp as she made her point. "Besides, this was my gift to give. It wasn't yours to take. And I wanted—no, I waited—to give it to you. I'm happy with my decision. Aren't you?"

He swallowed hard. Happy? Nah. This tenderness between them went far beyond such a temporary, mortal word. Eternal was a better definition for what they now shared. Celestial. "To hell and back," he said sincerely, suddenly as emotional as he'd ever been, while his rough, callused fingers combed through her lovely tangles. "I'd go to hell and back for you, Lass. You know that, don't you?"

Straightening, she canted her head to the side as if studying him. "This has been a long time coming, Ash."

"Aye," he nodded, his question still unanswered. "But a better home-*coming* I can nah imagine." Did he dare push the limit? His tongue scraped at the back of his teeth, eager to tell her, to say the words. The word. To be honest.

But a pensive light glowed in her eyes, turning them to pools of warm maple syrup and cautioning him to hold back. "I thought of you every day while I was gone, you know, trying to figure what to do with you. With us."

His heart melted. One glance over his belly to where she still sat with her legs spread and their bodies joined, and he teased, his voice as rough as fifty grit sandpaper. "I'd say you've come to the right conclusion." There was that magic word again. *Come.* It warmed him down to his toes.

"Have I, though? Is there any hope of this thing between us working, Ash, or are we kidding ourselves?" Colby flounced her shimmering locks to the side as she laid her head to his chest in a lovely womanly gesture, one he dared not take for submission. Not with her.

Ash fisted his hand in that blonde silk, addicted to the luxury of her body. With her breasts mashed to his belly, her nipples still pebbled and tempting, he could barely breathe. He'd expected her skin tone to be pale, more cream than mocha. But she was the lightest shade of brown sugar, as if she'd lost every last bit of pink pigmentation while baking in the Mideastern sun.

His nostrils flared, pulling in the warm rush of roses and gunpowder. Where she came up with a fragrance like that, he didn't know, but it fit his blonde-haired queen.

Ash swallowed hard, knowing full well their way forward would be rocky only because it had been in the past. He tended to boss her around; she tended to fight him when he did. Push and shove. They bickered, lost in an endless power struggle, her with her hell-bent need for independence, to be treated as an equal; him with his old-fashioned need to protect her from herself. To provide for her though he knew she was a capable, intelligent woman. And bloody strong.

Aye, Ash knew full well he was to blame. He had to let her go now just as when he'd prayed for her safe return home. She needed to live her life. He could not do it for her, nor force her to live like his mum. It wasn't in Colby to be less than who she was. No. 'Twas Ash Callahan who had to change. Swallowing hard, he vowed to be man enough to let her go—if that was what she wanted.

The dirt-poor son of an Irish sheep farmer didn't stand a chance of winning one of Boston's finest ladies anyway. Yet here he was, so hard in love with Colby that she made the pain in his soul seem a lighter burden to bear. He could do it—for her. He could let her fly—or fight—or whatever she thought she needed to do. He could be that man. The man she needed.

"I have nothing to give you," Ash bit out, smoothing his rough, callused hands over her shoulders, mapping her neck and spine. Colby might as well know that from the get-go. Poor or rich, he meant to claim her, then begin anew at rebuilding if she'd have him. Wasn't that what made America great, the stuff of poor men's dreams? Wasn't that what they were doing, even now? Starting over?

Her dainty fingers fluttered over his bicep, and damn. The male in him flexed at her light-as-a-butterfly touch like a schoolboy out to impress his girl.

"We live such different lives," she whispered to his chest.

Ash shook his head, not believing for a second that their differences would be their undoing. "Not if you're still the woman I fell in love with. You believe in yourself, do you nah?"

"Of course, but you're an artist while I'm the practical one. You dreamed impossible dreams while I went off to war and—"

That got his dander up. "Is that what this is about then, that you were man enough to fight for our country, while I was—?"

"Tsk, tsk, tsk. Honestly, don't be so defensive. You know that wasn't what I meant. I love you, Ash. I do, but is love enough?"

You love me? Didn't that one blessed word knock the wind out of his pretentious sails? By all the saints in heaven, he'd never thought he'd hear it from her mouth. It soothed like a balm from heaven, confirming the tender gift she'd just given him.

He cupped her hard head to his heart, so thankful. But she'd proclaimed her feelings so casually, as if her love for him was common knowledge between them when it wasn't. As if he'd already known, when he truly hadn't dared believe it could be so. "Look at me, Lass. Please. I need to see your pretty golden eyes."

Lifting her head, his heart skipped a thundering beat. There she lay in all her glory, her bare breasts blushed and plump on his chest, her nipples peaked and pointed at him, and the plump cheeks of her ass like two tawny mountains rising behind her. 'Twas like seeing the first sunrise in the Garden of Eden, with her face aglow as it was. Bright amber sparkles glittered from beneath her hooded eyelids. Her tongue slid over lush and swollen reddened lips. Colby had the rumpled look of a woman in love and it sent an instant message to his cock for...

More.

Unbidden, the randy thing hardened, eliciting another smile from the tigress in his arms. Threading his fingers through her hair, Ash tugged Colby forward until they were nose-to-nose and heart-to-heart. "I've loved you since the first day I saw you running through Faneuil Market, Lass. I love all you stand for and every last thing you fight for. But know this—I'll love you until the world burns to—"

"Ash?" Colby whispered, blinking like the tempting, but oh, so innocent seductress she was.

"Aye," he breathed, his soul finally at rest, and his dearest dream come true. "Love is enough. Trust me. 'Tis enough." *And so are you.*

Chapter Eighteen

The time for talk had come. They lay on Ash's couch, their legs intertwined, Colby's one knee over his, and his nose in her hair. He seemed to have a thing for her hair, threading a clump of it through his fingers, letting it fall only to lift it to his nose and start all over again.

They'd dressed as much as they were going to, him bare-chested in just jeans, unsnapped and the zipper half done; her in one of his Boston Red Sox baseball shirts. *Nothing more.*

After their first go round, they'd bathed in his

dime-sized bathtub; giggling like two teenagers at each other when the water cooled, and they couldn't turn the hot water faucet on with just their toes. He'd been so gentle, washing away the blood of her lost—and freely given virginity—before he'd let her step into the tub. For whatever reason, his hands on her there, between her legs, had felt protective and possessive, and she'd loved watching him take care of her.

It wasn't a big deal, yet—it was. The sight of him on his knees watered her eyes. He'd seemed intent on serving her. Being treasured like that and giving up her need to control everything, was an uncommon feeling for her. *Another first.*

After the bath, they went after each other again. His dining room table was rapidly cleared off and used until she'd squirmed and begged for release. The man did have a wicked tongue on him, and she liked it.

Ash was solid, built of coiled musculature that roped sturdy bones and tendons, comprising the perfect male specimen. Two tattoos marked his deeply tanned skin. A fine Celtic cross in a bracelet of shamrocks circled his right bicep. The outline of a fish, head up, tail down, the ancient symbol of Christianity, marked his left.

She couldn't keep her hands off of him, nor her tongue. Couldn't get enough of his salty male flavor. And that cologne he wore? It was fast becoming her favorite addiction.

Exploring his body was a sublime adventure, and she was on the safari of her life, her fingers strolling over his ribs, searching out the places that made him hiss, the hollows that caught his breath. Her palms mapped the solid six-pack that narrowed to a sculpted V. Wherever her fingertips and lips landed, she pinched, scraped, licked, and kissed.

Ash didn't sigh as much as growl when he was content, though often that growl simmered into a sensual, blood-boiling purr. It was odd how one little sound could incite another round of ferocious grappling and mind-blowing sex. But it did. It seemed they liked to wrestle, which explained how they'd gotten from the kitchen table to the couch. Next stop? His bed. Or so he'd said. There was still the hallway, and they hadn't done it standing up—yet.

Colby now knew the contours of his flat belly all the way to the juncture of his groin and the delightfully ticklish jut of his hips. Her fingertips strayed in abandon down that enticing trail of black crisp hairs below his navel. And lower. She did that just to hear the hitch in his breathing. To know she could make him shiver at her command.

Of all the warriors she'd worked alongside in the Army, the drill sergeants, commanding officers, and other Rangers, this gentle man had them beat. Struggling to keep her hands to herself, she balled her fist to his bare chest, where he captured it in his catchers' mitt-sized grip. How uncommonly small and dainty she felt curled into him, his free hand shaping the right cheek of her ass, massaging and squeezing. Warming.

They were back to discussing the arsonist.

"Trust me. If I catch him near my mom again, I'll end him," Colby declared, her head on the muscular pillow of his corded bicep.

Ash didn't answer, just "Hmmm."

She missed the scent of cigarettes though, the other dimension to her man. "Did you stop smoking?" *That'd be wonderful.*

The scruff on his chin scraped over her brow. "I only smoke at the pub. 'Tis a bad habit, but 'tis also a drinking thing."

The beat of his heart vibrated beneath their joined hands. "Tell me about Ireland. Where'd you live before you left home?"

There was that purr again. "Ah, I'm going to

take you there some day, you can be sure of that. Ireland is pure magic, and the more you believe in it, the happier you'll be there. Me family's farm's outside Newport in County Mayo, overlooking the Black Oak River."

"What'd you raise there?"

"Mostly rocks. Some sheep and cattle. More rocks."

That made her smile. She'd heard Ireland was known for its rock fences and walls, but she had yet to see for herself. "So why did you come to America? Did you stop believing in all that Celtic magic?"

His chin bumped her forehead. "You'll nah believe me, but I heard a call one day, a siren's call to leave home and go West. I'd fallen asleep in the field, watching sheep I was, but it woke me just the same. At first, I believed 'twas the wind, or maybe the fierce pirate queen, Grace O'Malley herself, come to roust me off her ancestral land."

When Colby pushed up on one elbow to read his eyes at this outlandish tale, he spiked a brow. "Ah, I see the disbelief in your eye, but trust me on this. Us Irish believe in witches and the banshee, in magic and destiny. 'Twas nah for me to ignore the whispering voice I heard."

She drummed her fingers over his right nipple,

teasing him as she suspected he was teasing her. "Why would Grace O'Malley call you out? Were you living in her castle or something?"

Ash wrinkled his nose as if she was the one stretching the truth. "Rockfleet Castle is a tourist trap, Lass. There'd be no living in it. 'Tis a bloody tower of cold stone. A fortress. The only part fit for habitation is the very top floor, where no woman in her right mind would willingly dwell. What do you take me for, a monk?"

She had to laugh. "Not after what we just did to each other on your dining room table, no. You're no monk." Colby sank her chin to his chest, wanting to know everything. "Tell me more."

The big, warm hand on her ass slid up to the back of her head. "I truly believed I heard something that day. It might have been the three bottles of the black beer from the night before. It might've been Da calling. But it told me very clearly that me heart lay west, that me time had come. That there was nothing in Ireland for a drunken carpenter." He shrugged, lifting her head with his chest. "So here I am."

She thought she heard a pensive tone to this tale. "What did the voice say, the exact words?"

His heartbeat kicked up a notch. "Me name, as clear as a bell. 'Ash.' Then the wind whispered, 'C-C-Colby... Col-be-e-e...'"

Okay, that made her laugh. She landed an open-handed smack to his furrowed stomach and giggled. "Liar. No Irish pirate queen told you to come to Boston because of me."

"No, but I did come to Boston, and the day I spotted you running through Faneuil Hall in nothing but skin-tight boy shorts and a sports bra—"

Another smack. "That's how you knew I had a mole, isn't it?"

A deep throaty chuckle sounded from his throat. "'Twas also when I knew I'd come to the right country. You and your girlfriend ran by me with nary a second look. It hurt me Irish pride, so I followed you all the way to Beacon Hill. You ran me legs off that day, woman, but you never knew I was behind you gasping like a bloody fish out of water."

"Hmmm. I did hear a lot of perverse panting behind me that day. I thought it was some stalker, but that was you, huh?"

A stinging swat landed on her ass. "I do nah think so. I was too far behind for you to have heard me, though 'twas a lovely view."

"So why the naked figurehead?"

Releasing her hand on his chest, he spread his fingers and lifted them to her view. "That part is real. When I was a boy, Da told me that magic lay in me hands, but there's no thirst for that sort of talent in Ireland. No need. But once I landed in Boston and found me first customer, me life fell into a cadence, a rhythm if you will. Before I knew it, I had orders coming out me ears. I leased a bigger place to carve, then diversified into chairs and chests to support me carving habit. People love a solid piece of wooden furniture, especially if the workmanship is quality. Soon, I needed more room, so I bought a warehouse."

He still hadn't answered her question. "The one that burned?"

"Aye, but that was nah the beginning of me bad luck. That started when you joined the Army."

That caught her attention. "How so?"

"'Twas then I lost me passion. I drank a wee bit too much. I lost a few customers."

By then she was leaning on his chest, her chin on the back of her flattened hand. "Okay, so I joined the Army." *That conversation's better left for another day.* "That still doesn't explain the nautical figureheads."

Tucking his chin to his chest, he looked her in the eye. "Because when I began carving you, everything came together for me again. I poured me heart into remembering every last detail. I didn't want to forget a thing." Leaning forward, Ash planted a warm, moist kiss in the center of her forehead. "Nah a single thing."

CHAPTER NINETEEN

Colby woke with her face mashed into a cushion, the room as dark as sin. The blackness of it slithered around her neck like an evil snake, coiled and smelling of sand and blood, blowback and sweat. How many coils that serpent had, she didn't know, but in the end, it would hiss and then it would strike. And when it did, men always died...

Afraid to move but needing with all her heart to run—to live!—she exploded to her knees, and just as quickly pushed to her feet. Guys should be bellowing by now. There should be more noise.

More panic than just hers.

Dizzy, with her fists cocked and her heart popping off adrenaline bursts designed to save or kill, her blood pressure spiked into a solid number ten migraine. Colby stood stock still, waiting for the click and hiss of an explosive beneath her feet.

From out of nowhere, a deep male voice rumbled, "Lass, what's wrong?"

"S-s-snake," she threw at him, the fool. What was *Ash* doing here? Now she had to protect *him* and *them* and... *Where's my fucking knife?*

Colby crouched, frantic for the ankle holster she wasn't wearing. Another burst of adrenaline and acid filled her gut. She stabbed stiff fingers into her hair, scared okay? Just gawddamned scared! *You can't kill what you can't see!*

Out of the rustling dark, warm hands descended softly to her shoulders. Fighting the need to scream, she allowed them to tug her up from the floor and into—Ash. Unable to hide her tremors, she barreled into that bare wall of muscle, clinging to him even as her hands tucked into his chest. That damned snake couldn't get her now, not with the sheer mass of this guy's body surrounding her. Shielding her. Whispering *'there, there'* at the side of her out-of-control, bobbing head while he cradled her. All of her.

"I've got you," Ash soothed, his breath warm in her ear, his body cocooning hers even as her bones and teeth rattled, the top of her head bumping his chin. "'Tis just the rain."

But Colby was never afraid of inclement weather. "Light," she hissed. "Turn on the damned light."

Lifting her off the floor, he sank back onto the couch. The lamp on the end table clicked on as Ash pressed her tough, lean fighting machine of a body into his. And she let him.

"I've got you now," he murmured, as gentle as Colby had never heard him. "What's got your heart pounding so hard, Lass? Take a deep breath before you give yourself a stroke."

Ashamed and embarrassed, she swallowed hard, her Mean Bitch cover blown for good. But how to tell him about this kind of bone-numbing fear? She wasn't truly afraid of snakes or the giant spiders she'd seen in the desert. It made no sense, but somehow her brain had transformed RPGs and IEDs into serpents of flying, slithering death, the kinds of lethality that lay hidden under sand and dirt until good men with loving families back home stepped in the wrong place. Until bodies blew apart and entrails flew like—snakes.

"It's nothing," she lied, panting still. *Nothing but my mixed-up brain on crack.*

She hadn't realized how much she hated the dark until the lights went out one night in Cambodia. In heart-pumping frenzy, she'd beat feet to her neighbor's apartment, a good thing since he ended up being Smoke Montoya, an ex-Navy SEAL who didn't ask questions. Just gave her a safe place—with lights—to crash for the night.

The next day she'd lied and told him her toilet was broke. He'd shrugged and offered his couch for however long she needed it. Like a gruff teddy bear, Smoke Montoya let her bully him into letting her stay, but she suspected he knew the real reason. Yeah, guys like him knew damned well how dark the night could be. Maybe that was why he'd always kept a light on, too? *Hmmmmm.*

When Ash pressed a kiss to the top of her head, Colby let the truth out. "I sleep with a nightlight," she whispered, only going to say it once. She—a tougher- than-tough Army Ranger— was afraid of the dark. If the guys from her squad could see her now.

"Then from now on you'll be sleeping with me," Ash said with a crack in that big gruff, tender voice, his fingers still cupping the back of her head, holding her close.

He couldn't have said anything better. The tension eased out of her even as her tired eyes brimmed with tears she'd never let fall.

Colby swallowed hard, needing to explain. "They kill them all," she began quietly, wiping the tears and snot off her face against her bicep in one stealthy move. "Women and babies. Little boys and girls. Men. Husbands and fathers and..." A wicked shudder got the best of her. "...grandfathers. Grandmothers. For no better reason than because they're assholes."

Ash tipped forward and back, rocking as if she were a little girl and understanding her mixed pronouns. "Aye, terrorists," he breathed. "They're everywhere."

"Yeah, terrorists." Nodding, Colby loosened her grip on his poor chest muscles. Another gulp and she licked her lips, her knees still curled against his belly. "You never know when the next hit will come. Just when you think you're safe—"

"You're nah," he finished for her. "I'm from Ireland, remember? We have our own home-grown version, who've been killing good people for years."

Oddly, that, along with everything else she

knew about Ash, helped. Deliberately, Colby drew in a deep breath and let it go through her nostrils.

Another warm kiss melted into her hair. "'Tis safe here, love," he purred. "Sleep now. I'll take the first watch."

Colby couldn't place the song vibrating beneath her ear. It sounded sad and happy at the same time, and she realized that maybe, just maybe, she was safe for the first time in years. Not only safe but wanted.

CHAPTER TWENTY

When Irish Eyes are smiling,

Sure 'tis like a morn in Spring...

Like a warning, the song his mum used to sing to him as a little boy, ran in one continual loop in Ash's mind. He hadn't been this at peace with the world of men since, well, since he'd left that field alongside the Black Oak River and cast his dreams to the westward blowing wind.

Somewhere in his storytelling tonight, he'd told Colby how the figureheads turned a pretty penny, and that they—she—had saved him from going daft. That much was true. Yet even now, when he knew how fractured her spirit was, he could nah go on with his lies to protect her. She needed to know.

As if she agreed with him in her sleep, Colby rubbed her cheek against his bare chest like a satisfied cat that had returned home to a warm hearth. And Ash was happy just to hold his fierce warrior princess and pet her while she slept. To love her.

In the lilt of Irish laughter

You can hear the angels sing...

Aye, but 'twasn't angels singing that Ash had heard. If anything, he dared not fall asleep, not with some insane killer on the loose and Colby's fear of the dark fresh in his mind. He kept his ears tuned to the sounds from the street or the softest touch at his doorknob or window. His eyes strained to decipher every shadow flickering across his windows, and his nostrils flared to detect the slightest hint of petrol.

His love for Colby knew no bounds, but the news Kevin had shared earlier made for an incredibly anxious midnight hour. Not only did he worry about Colby, Bella, and Tula, but now he feared for the dockworkers who handled overseas containers, too. That was where the first three fires had broken out, on the docks where the containers storing his *alleged* orders had been stacked pending pick-up.

Which meant the arsonist knew him and his friends, his business and his personal habits, not only enough to sabotage him, but to frame him as well. Earlier, Ash had feigned a calm demeanor to settle her down. Colby didn't need more grief in her life. But now he worried as the song in his head ragged on.

When Irish hearts are happy,

All the world seems bright and gay...

Gay nothing. A world filled with the likes of Colby Quaid should shine, not be as dark and sinister as the one now besmirched with the soot and smoldering embers of a murderer with a blowtorch. Ash pressed her warm, limp body to his chest, her head under his chin, duty bound to make this world safe for her.

He pressed one of many anxious kisses to her brow, pleased they'd had this one perfect night together. But the new day's sun would soon be spreading through his east-facing kitchen window, and the fact remained. Someone in Beantown was out to get him.

The bloody truth he'd meant to tell Colby before she'd fallen asleep was not as romantic as he'd made it sound earlier. It was much more sinister. His older brother, Liam, did not tend sheep on the hillside, nor did he milk any dairy herd. Quite the opposite. Liam led the local band of the *Óglaigh na hÉireann,* the bloody *Warriors of Ireland,* a splinter group off the Irish Republican Army.

Aye, the *Óglaigh na hÉireann* did rare good deeds on a rarer day. Occasionally, when it suited them, they sought out and meted justice to drug dealers and underground slave traders, child smugglers, and the like. But more often, they used violence to further their political agenda. They were behind several recent bombings in Belfast and abroad. Innocent people had died, and Ash could not abide by that lawless code. Not for anything.

He hadn't gotten involved with the *Warriors,* but Liam had. Guilt by association ate at Ash until the day he'd fallen asleep after a drunken binge in the field. When he woke, he knew he had to leave the country he loved, or be sucked into a life of sin, crime, and intrigue at Liam's insistent bullying.

Gods bless her, it was his dead mother's tearful voice he'd heard that day in the field, not some Irish banshee or mystical pirate queen. In her simple Irish way, Annie Callahan had distinctly told him to, "Leave now, before he ruins you, too." 'Course, she'd said it in Gaelic, but you get the drift.

So Ash had left Liam and the infamous *Óglaigh na hÉireann* behind. When the cruise to America was done, he'd ended up a pauper in Boston. He'd already lost everything. Fresh off the boat and with not coins in his pocket, he'd spent the first few nights in his new country sleeping on the docks, rousted by many an Irish cop until the night Officer Declan MulCahey introduced him to the warm beds and hot meals at Sister Bernadette's homeless shelter. The good people there gave him a change of clothes, a shower, and a hearty clap of encouragement on the back. In two days he'd been hired to drive trucks for a freight company. In a month's time, he'd saved enough money to rent a flat in Southie. Month by month and paycheck by paycheck, he'd prospered.

Pressing another kiss to her forehead, Ash knew he needed to be honest with Colby. He was no simple woodcarver from the Emerald Isle. He'd changed his name when he came to America, but he was Ash O'Callaghan, brother of the notorious, Liam O'Callaghan. He might even be a wanted man.

And when Irish eyes are smiling

Sure, they steal your heart away...

Only Ash's Irish eyes weren't smiling. They were crying.

CHAPTER TWENTY-ONE

The lamp was still on. Colby nose twitched to the comforting aroma of coffee. Other delicious scents, too. Oak shavings. The wind off the harbor. Rain falling. And—*thank you, Jesus*—Ash. Now her favorite aroma.

She spiked a handful of fingers into her tangled locks, raking them out of her eyes and off her face. It took a second to realize entirely too much of her bare ass-end was showing. Along with her pride. Groggy from her over-the-top panic attack during the night, she yanked her shirt down and spit lint off her tongue.

"Ash?" she called out quietly in case he'd left her for the comfort of his bed, the bed she had yet to see. But he wouldn't do that, not after what she'd confided in him, would he?

"Here, Lass" he called from his kitchen.

Great, he's been looking at my bare ass all morning. How long have I been mooning him? He should've at least covered her. About then, she spied the blanket lying on the floor alongside the couch. *Oh. He did. Well, okay then.*

"What time is it?" she asked as she climbed to her feet and gave her hips a very un-Colby-like girly-wiggle that made her breasts bounce. With one hand in her hair still taming the rats' nests, she wandered around the corner and into the alcove that passed for a kitchen. What a sight to behold, her man in a ragged pair of jeans that looked soft to the touch, a simple white t-shirt stretched over a rippling wall of chest muscles. *I could look at him all day and not have my fill.*

His brows lifted when he spied her. Manly appraisal dropped to her bare feet, then began a slow, soul-burning perusal up her body, pausing at the hem of her shirt. Assessing. Blue eyes glowed. They lingered at her jutting breasts. Who knew horny nipples acted like this? Pebbled nothing. They were stretched out, reaching for his wicked lips, needing another bite or pinch.

Nearly undone by that lusty, feral shadow shifting over his ruggedly handsome face, she crossed her arms as if that action wouldn't lift those girls up like plump offerings on a serving tray just for him. Which they most definitely were. *Let him look.*

When that same breathtaking smile curved the corners of his delicious mouth, the impulse to run to him ambushed Colby so hard that she stuck a fist in the edge of her—*his*—shirt, pulling it down instead of tearing it off and going at him again. Would he mind if she climbed all over him in his kitchen? She doubted it.

Rapping his knuckles to the short breakfast bar, he cleared his throat. "Take a seat. We need to talk."

His tone brooked no debate, so she plopped her now covered ass to the only stool in the place, hooked her toes over the lowest rung, and leaned over the steaming cup of coffee waiting for her at the bar. No man had ever made coffee for her before.

Closing her eyes, Colby took a sip of the richest, creamiest brew she'd ever tasted. A genuine sigh breathed out of her and every last bit of her tension from last night's terrors evaporated. "What brand is this?" she asked.

Not since she'd left Texas had she had a decent cup. When her life settled down, the first thing on her Christmas list was a Keurig with all the options.

"You like that, eh?" He cocked a salacious grin that tightened every last one of her core muscles.

"Oh, yes."

Colby could see herself moving in with Ash, maybe not into this tiny flat, but somewhere. Together. Maybe closer to town. Near her mother and Tula. At least where she could get her hands on him any time, any day.

"Ready?"

She drew in a deep breath of her coffee, then opened her eyes. "Ready for...?"

"Another story," he said, his voice just as firm, his eyes still locked on hers but the sparkle in his eyes dimmed.

Colby gathered the cup to her lips for another sip. "There hasn't been another arson, has there?"

"No more fires, but the truth, love. Just the truth." Ash set his cup firmly to the counter. "'Tis nah the whole story I told you last night, and I'll nah have our life together, if there's to be one, fettered with deceit. If we're going to do this, we need to be honest with each other from day one. 'Tis a rule I broke last night, but I'll nah be breaking it again. Of that you can be sure."

Okay, now Colby was worried. She had been away too long. Was there another woman in his life? "You already know I'm afraid of the dark. Just say it then. Spit it out."

A smile creased his brow, and the light in his eyes flashed back to life. "You're nah afraid of anything, love. You're just reacquainting yourself with normalcy, that's all. Take a deep breath and forgive yourself for being human. I've had me own bad days when I've hated the dark. I'll remember to leave a light on from now on, deal?"

That sounded promising. *No other woman then. Okay.* Colby dragged an embarrassed hand through her hair, wishing she had an elastic to keep it out of her face. Morning after hair—*ugh.* "Deal. So what's so important?"

He folded his arms and leaned over the bar. "I didn't lie last night, but there's more to the telling of what I told you. 'Twas nah the Irish queen I heard in me da's field that last day. 'Twas me own dear mother, Annie. I heard her as clear as the summer wind whistling off the limestone cut of the Burrin." *There was that brogue again.* "She told me to leave before he ruined me too, he being Liam, me brother. And that's another thing. Me name is nah Callahan. 'Tis O'Callaghan." He paused as if that name should mean something to her. "'Tis Ó Ceallacháin in Gaelic."

Oh, that. "So?" she asked, loving how the Irish rolled off his tongue, especially since he'd not confided in her like this before. "Lots of people Americanize their names when they come here, Ash. No big deal." She kept her tone calm, cool, and civil. Hopeful.

His jaw squared. "O'Callaghan, as in Liam O'Callaghan." Again he paused, raking her with sharp eyes beneath those intense brows.

"Oh, no," she lifted her fingers to her lips in mock feminine dismay. "Not Liam O'Callaghan, the Irish terrorist?"

Ash didn't get her attempt at humor. Instead, honest anguish glimmered in his deep blues, tempting Colby to be as straight with him as he'd been with her, and to lay all her cards on the table. *Just not yet...*

"Aye, and I'm sorry from the bottom of me heart, love. I'll understand if you need to hit me or scream. I deserve it. I might not've lied to you, but I wasn't forthcoming, and I should've been. The honest truth? Liam's me older brother, and the bloody reason Mum and Da died. He brought his politics and his war to their front door the day he and his boys bombed the constabulary in Belfast."

"So Liam's not on the family farm tending sheep?" She couldn't resist one last dig. He'd expect that from her.

Ash's cheeks ballooned with a mighty breath before a sigh hollowed them. "I have no idea where he is. We haven't kept in touch, nah since the day he tried to recruit me, and I told him to crawl back to Hell, that he'd caused enough pain and despair."

Colby set her cup to the counter, unwilling to bait this poor man any longer. His distress at losing his parents radiated through every word. The truth was out now. "I know."

Ash canted his head nearly forty-five degrees to his left shoulder, his brows as wrinkled as his nose. "Excuse me? You know what?"

Lifting her cup back to her lips, Colby took a sip before she admitted, "Army Rangers have top-secret security clearance. I've been through a very thorough and intrusive background check. I found all about Liam when I listed you as a personal reference. I'm sorry for what he did to your family. You must hate him."

His lips puckered with a snort. "Aye, but you let me think...? You let me go on and...? How long?"

Ah, the coffee tasted good, but so did this particular moment when she had the mighty glib tongue of Ash Callahan—O'Callaghan—tied in knots. "Actually, I've known for years."

He spread his legs wide, his head bowed to the counter and shaking. "I should've known I could nah hide this from the United States government. Am I nah the luckiest man alive?"

Colby slipped off the stool and rounded the bar, elbowing her way under his arm. Lifting to her toes, she pressed her palms to his shaven cheeks. "I'd love you no matter what the Army dug up on your brother, Ash O'Callaghan," she assured him, loving the feel of his skin under her fingertips. "If it helps, there was nothing on you not even a parking ticket. What can I do to make it better?"

"Callahan," he corrected, a growl of pride in his tone. "I'm an American now." With a rumbling growl, he snagged her off her feet and set her on the bar, a predatory gleam in his eyes as he wedged his belly between her knees. "And there's nothing to be done for me, but my, you're a wee one for one so brave."

Colby threaded her fingers over his head, still careful of the burns on his neck, but sure he knew her sex was bared to him, the wicked tease. "Aye," she breathed, loving him with every beat of her heart. "Now show me your bedroom, Ash. I'll be taking my second cup of coffee in there."

No sooner said than he palmed her backside and lifted her against him. "Aye, and maybe I'll enjoy a wee spot of breakfast, too."

Colby caught the wolfish gleam in his eye. She wrapped her arms around his ribs, in love with being in love with Ash. Somehow, he'd sanded her rough edges away, and she was on her way to heaven. She would've gotten there, too, if her cell phone hadn't rung.

"Blimey, where'd you leave it?" he asked, annoyance crisp in his voice as he dodged the shoes and clothes scattered on his living room floor.

"In my jeans pocket. Over there." *With my knife.* Colby pointed toward the other end of the couch where she'd last seen her clothes. "It's probably just Mom or Tula wondering where I am this morning. Darn, I should've called them last night so they wouldn't worry. I'll be quick."

"Jesus, Mary, and Joseph, what a mess. You'd

think someone had a magnificent orgy in here." Ash had the nerve to grin even as his deft fingers kneaded her ass, driving her wild. "Can you reach it, love?"

He tipped her backward, but it was hard to stretch with his mouth nuzzling her neck, his tongue tracing a line of molten lust over the sensitive flesh of her breast. Shivers skittered up her spine and those damned nipples hardened. Could he feel them through her shirt?

"Don't drop me," Colby warned even as she giggled, loving his hands on her.

"Farther," he urged, his mouth now firmly suckling the top of her breast, where he'd surely left a nice red raspberry. "Just let go of me and grab your pants. Trust me, love. I won't drop you."

Laughing, Colby let loose of him and fell backward, arching for her pants even as Ash smoothed one hand up her back to balance her. The nerve. He tugged her shirt up with his teeth, still on his way to her nipples, not that she minded.

"Ash!" she squealed, the phone ringing again, and her body now hot and wet for him.

At last. Colby snagged her jeans up from the floor and tugged the phone free of her pocket. "H-hello?" The smile spread over her lips made her stutter. Or maybe it was Ash rubbing his whiskers between her breasts, while he purred with outright male satisfaction.

"Colby?" Tula barked. "Of course, it's you. That's who I called. Is Bella with you?"

CHAPTER TWENTY-TWO

Ash didn't like it, not one bit. Colby had gone back to Beacon Hill looking for her mum, while he canvassed the streets closest to the harbor looking for Bella. The daft woman had been told to stay put in her hotel room. Could none of the Quaid women do what they were told? *Obviously not!*

Bella was Colby's mother after all. Like daughter, like mother. Or was it the other way around? He didn't know any more, but they were both driving him to the edge of insanity this morn. Bella, because he could nah find her! Colby, because she wasn't with him where she should've been, damn her obstinate ass.

With every blind alley and dead end, his angst ramped up. Didn't matter, wherever she was, he couldn't protect her, and with his brother possibly now in the picture, Ash very much needed to know precisely where Colby was. Right this very minute!

The police had been alerted and were looking for Bella. Back toward the harbor Ash stalked, his eyes and ears tuned toward the sight or sound of a pigheaded woman in a powder-blue turban and a bed jacket. That should've made Bella easy to spot, but was it? Not so much. Bloody hell, he'd even checked the Boston T's Downtown, South, and Harbor Street train stations. No luck.

The only thing happening in the city today was the impending sense of doom gripping the back of his neck like the sharpened claws of a schoolmarm from hell. He could nah shake the disquiet that Liam was behind all of this, the arson fires and Bella's vanishing act included. 'Twould be like Liam to stalk the people who meant everything to Ash. To strike at the heart of him. It'd kill Colby if anything happened to her mum.

"Bollocks!" he hissed, his head lowered and glaring at the world from behind his thick brows. What should've been a merry day in bed with the lady of his heart was now spent combing the streets in panic.

'Bella can nah have gotten this far,' he thought grimly, 'nah as old as she is.'

So where was she then? Who'd lured her out of the hotel to begin with? All Tula knew was she'd been in the shower when the phone rang. By the time she'd toweled off and stuck her head out the bathroom door, the hotel room was wide open, and Bella and Pierre were gone. At first blush, Tula thought Bella had simply gone to catch that dastardly cat of hers, that they both might be wandering the floor in search of each other. Not so.

With determination, Ash's legs ate up the sidewalk to Long Wharf and its steady crowd of tourists. It'd be easy to get lost there, or simply turned around in Bella's case. She *was* a pint low in her thinking.

At the corner of State and Atlantic he saw her—*thank God!*—sitting across the busy way under several shade trees that lined the dock. She didn't look hurt, more baffled was all. Watching the tourists stroll by and waving. Smiling.

Fluttering her fingers on her knees, then ducking her shoulders as if she were nothing more than a little lost girl.

Which in some ways, she was. The sight tore at him. Bella was more daft than he'd suspected. Well, he had her now. Against the green light Ash ran, dodging cars, bikers, and the ever-present power walkers America was known for, to reach Bella before he lost sight of her.

"Bella!" Ash called out, waving frantically.

The silly woman waved back, a vacant smile on her face that scared him to death.

At last he crouched at her knee, breathing hard but not wanting to frighten her. "Everyone's been looking for you, love. What are you doing here?"

She peered at him, her sweet face crinkled and her brows knitted. "You're sure a handsome man. Do I know you?" she asked with her nose up.

"Yes, Mum, you do. I'm Ash Callahan, your daughter's friend. Colby sent me to find you. She's worried out of her mind, Mum."

Bella shook her head, several wiry grays hairs coming loose from the turban. "You're wrong. Colby left me. She's in the Army now."

"No, she came home to see you and..." He tried again, frustrated at her forgetfulness. "I carried you out of the fire at your home yesterday. Remember?"

She must have. Bella's gaze flitted over his shoulder to the tourists behind him, the ones coming from the same part of town where he'd just searched high and low for her. "I can't leave. Not yet. She told me to wait right here, said she'd be right back." Bella's gnarled fingertips set to drumming on her knees again. She seemed to be unraveling as quickly as her turban.

He scanned the tourists for anyone headed in Bella's direction. "Who told you to wait?"

"That woman." Bella fluttered her fingers at him dismissively. "You know. That... woman."

He didn't have a clue what Bella thought she knew. "What'd she look like? Can I help you find her?" he asked kindly as he captured Bella's hand in his. Man, it was as cold as ice.

Another headshake and her gaze made a nervous dart to busy Atlantic Avenue. "She's a tiny thing, but she's very strong. She's got gorgeous hair. Her head is covered in ringlets, but I didn't catch her name," Bella admitted with a crack in her voice as she patted her turban with her other hand. "She never told me her name, but she said she knew me, and she wanted to show me something." One balled fist went to Bella's mouth, now bracketed in worry. "Oh, dear. Do you think she's lost? She said she'd be right back, but it's been while."

Without releasing her fingers, Ash dragged his cell phone from his jean's pocket with his free hand. The sound of Colby's voice would surely soothe her mum's nerves. "Aye, she might have gotten lost. How about I wait here with you until she comes back?" he asked, Colby's number ringing in his ear. "While we wait, I'll get you a nice lemonade or an ice."

The phone kept ringing.

Bella brightened. "I have a cat you know," she said cheerily, the smile on her face as innocent as a newborn babe's. "He's such a rascal, but I love my Pierre's wicked ways."

"Aye, you're a rascal, too, but a prettier one."

"She has the most peculiar cape," Bella blurted, her head cocked as if she'd just remembered the detail.

At last. Something to go on. "A cape you say? What color? How tall was she? What color hair does your new friend have?"

That same tired, daft smile curved the corners of her lips. Bella shook her fingers out of his grip and cupped his chin. "Blue, I think. Her eyes were blue like yours." The poor thing looked so mixed up and— "She kept singing that silly song."

Okay, now we're getting somewhere. "What song?" he asked, needing Bella to focus.

Her head bobbed to the right, then the left as she hummed some old nursery song Ash couldn't place. This was getting him nowhere. Still crouched there on the sidewalk with one elbow to his knee, Ash pivoted on the ball of his boot, scanning the sidewalk with fear alive in his heart. Colby hadn't answered as she'd promised. Why was that no surprise?

Acid pumped like a fire hose in his gut. This was a set up. Some woman with blue eyes— maybe— wearing a cape—maybe—had intentionally lured Bella into the street for one of two reasons, either to kill her, or to get Colby out in the open. But why?

He swallowed hard. *Where the feckin' hell are you, Liam? I know 'tis you. Show yourself. You and your latest treacherous girlfriend. I know you're out there.*

Colby finally answered, only she didn't. "If you've reached this recording, it means I'm too busy to talk right now. Take a chance. Leave a message. I might call back, but then again..."

Ash waited the pre-requisite number of heartbeats to the beep. "Call me, darlin'," he begged. "I found your mum. She's safe, but Colby. Liam's behind all of this. I'm sure of it. Call me!"

She couldn't get her bearings, not with her head pounding like some FNG, as in some fucking new guy, had launched an M320, 40mm grenade launcher inside of her skull. Christ, it was dark where she sat. Shivery dark. Not a speck of light shone anywhere.

Leaning her forehead to her wrists, which were bound together with what felt like one of those damned plastic zip-ties, and were also lifted and secured to something that felt like a cold pipe over her head, Colby growled. *She'd been blindsided. Now she was a prisoner. The nerve.*

It was cool and dank, like basement or old cellar dank, in this... this... wherever she was. Not a wine cellar kind of cool though, more like dirt and wet concrete cool. Her nostrils flared. Maybe urinal cool, too.

Something with icky, sticky feet skittered up her bare ankle. Before she had time to react, it dived off her knee and scurried away. Creeped out now, goosebumps raced up the back of her neck.

Somehow, she'd lost her shoes. Colby couldn't remember how or where. But damn it to hell, no Ranger worth her salt would've let herself be knocked senseless, kidnapped, and restrained like this.

Shit. She swallowed hard, face to face with not a glimmer of light except for an occasional twinkle at her peripheral, most likely the result of being bludgeoned. It didn't get any better than this, being scared of the dark—in the dark—with a rat and a possible concussion.

"I want my gun," she told the blackness enveloping her, but her voice came out timid and quivering. Whoever'd kidnapped her now had her weapon, damn them. Rubbing her ankles together, she felt her knife holster, unreachable for the moment, but there, thank God. "But I still want my gun."

The icky thing with sticky feet came back, but this time Colby was ready for it. Cocking her knee, she gave it her best soccer kick, a well-timed toe shot, with a vehement, "Get the hell away from me!"

Away it sailed with a shrill squeak before it hit something solid—like a wall, but awfully close. Heart pounding now, Colby twisted her neck to take stock of the prison she couldn't see, which was beginning to feel more like a closet. A too small closet with a rat. Or rats.

She didn't get the sense of there being much air in here, but neither could she see anything but inky black darkness. "Damn it, who's out there? Who did this to me?"

Like radar, the volume and tone of her voice brought scary information back to her. She was right. There was no echo. No depth. The space she was trapped in sounded hollow and small. Isolated. Traffic rumbled from a not too distant street. Car horns honked. She could smell exhaust fumes even as the ground vibrated from the engine of a large truck, maybe a bus. Not a train though, and that was some relief.

Using her bound wrists to pull herself up to her knees, Colby's forehead met the low ceiling with a bump and a well-earned, "Son-of-a-bitch!"

Don't panic. Isn't that what everyone said before they started screaming?

Rattled to her core, Colby drew in a deep breath and exhaled slowly, trying to calm her heart rate. She would NOT dissolve into tears and hysteria. This unfortunate kidnapping would not be the end of her. Not her.

Think. What happened? How'd I get here?

She recalled running up her mother's front steps, ripping the police-tape out of her way before she'd unlocked the door and shoved her way inside. Admittedly, she'd been in a hurry with her mother missing. She'd wanted her pistols and enough ammo to confront Ash's terrorist brother if he were truly the one behind Bella's mysterious disappearance.

Colby knew now she should've been more cautious of running straight inside. But she hadn't. Home had always been safe. She'd never thought for one second it wasn't still. She'd barely slipped out of her shoes, not wanting to track anymore dirt through the place when someone struck her from behind and down she went.

Then, nothing until she woke up a prisoner. But the truth was that someone had been in her mother's house waiting for her. She'd been set up. Was that asshole Liam? If he'd set the fires like Ash thought, then yes, he was behind this kidnapping, possibly Bella's disappearance, too.

You ass! You ambushed me! Me! A highly trained Army Ranger. How pathetic is that?

"You'd better not hurt my mom, because I promise, Liam. When I get out of here, I'm going to kick your ass!" she yelled to the ceiling, hoping he could hear her.

In times of stress and losing streaks, she'd found that boisterous defiance actually helped. But God. Liam.

CHAPTER TWENTY-THREE

Kevin finally showed, but Ash was tired of waiting for someone to come up with a better plan than walking the streets and searching for Colby. He'd brought Bella back to her hotel, but on their way back, he was met by two of Boston's finest before he'd crossed John Fitzgerald Surface Road. Officers McKinley and Trask talked his ear off while they escorted him and Bella to safety, but they'd asked good questions, too.

By the time he hit the doors of the hotel, they knew all about Liam O'Callaghan and his terrorist ways, only none of those good questions or answers had located Colby, had they?

"Stop yer pacing," Kevin said quietly. "I've men on the streets and the boys in blue are searching. They'll find her." He hadn't moved from the chair by the window since he'd joined the wait, nor would he. Kevin was too good a friend to leave Ash to face this nightmare alone, but 'twas obvious the stress was wearing on him. Poor bloke looked as if he hadn't slept a wink.

Ash rolled the despair off his blistered neck. Again. He'd lost everything over these past few years, he didn't intend to lose Colby, too. But who could the woman in the cape have been, if she weren't a figment of Bella's dementia? That was the question Ash could not answer. Had Liam recruited his entire gang to America? For the love of Mike, was he even behind any of this? The not knowing was the worst part of the waiting.

Ash clenched his fists tight. He needed to hit something at the thought of Liam in Boston. Every call to his brother's phone had gone to voicemail, as had every call to Colby's gone to hers. Not that the odd coincidence meant anything, but it bloody well could.

Liam had always been the dark son in the

family, the one who'd never stopped until he had what he wanted. He wouldn't stop now. Even as a boy, he'd been the ne'er-do-gooder, the liar, and the cheat. The thieving scoundrel who had no problem breaking his mother's heart—or burning her home to the ground with her in it.

How many times over the years had Ash covered for him? Too many, and Ash regretted now every single instance of what he'd thought then was brotherly love. 'Twas Liam who'd driven his parents to their early graves. Liam who thought the world owed him, and Liam who always did as he'd please. 'Twould be a cold day in Hell he did the same to Colby.

But wishes were a lazy man's way of planning for his future, like believing he didn't need fire insurance. Ash knew better now. He would not be that lazy man again. The only way to best Liam was to strike back. If only he could find, the bloody bastard.

Liam's last words hadn't been kind. They'd fought fisticuffs that day at the farm, half in, half out of the river. Sheep scattered, and aye, Ash got his arse handed to him, but before Liam kicked muck into his face and walked away, he'd also promised, "I'll kill you the next time we meet, brother. Go on, Ash! Move to America like the feckin' coward you are! You think I can nah reach you there?" He'd spat the blood out of his mouth on Ash then. "And when you do, I'll follow and kill every last thing or person you love."

The vile memory demanded another pass through the gilded suite that Bella's lofty position in society had afforded her. Once around the settee in her lavish sitting room, then through a kitchen his entire flat would've fit in without crowding the walls. Circles. Ash was literally walking in circles with no end in sight and nowhere to go.

"Come on, have a chair," Kevin offered again. "You're wearing a path in the carpet and you'll make yourself sick if you keep this up."

Ash glared at his friend. "I am sick, you *eejit!*" he hissed. "This is me fault. Whoever started those fires is after me, nah Colby! Don't you understand? I've caused this. If it's Liam—"

"You don't know if he's even in the country."

"Then who is doin this?" Ash roared, his last nerve frazzled. "Who else could it be? Who else hates me enough to burn Boston to the ground to get at me?" *Of course it's Liam.*

"We don't know for certain this is even related to you." The man sounded tired and spent, but had Kevin forgotten?

"Like hell," Ash spat. "Your own department was building a case against me, remember? Don't lie to me, nah now. I know too much." *And yet I know nothing at all. But someone does.* "Give me the name of that insurance investigator, Kev. Do you have it on you?"

Kevin patted his chest pocket, then nodded as he pulled out a business card. "Here. Give him a call, but I promise you, he's not a pleasant chap to chat with, especially today."

"Why?"

"Because I challenged his findings this morning. I gave him names, Ash, character witnesses willing to vouch for you, and it was a long list. I told him he's got nothing to charge you with, but the bugger said he's got all he needs to put you in jail."

"He still thinks I'm the arsonist?" It made no sense. "All he's got is circumstantial evidence, and that won't stand up in court. What's his bloody name?"

Kevin sighed. "It's on the card."

Ash took the chair opposite Kevin's and dialed a Mr. Giles Bottomly of Leviathan Mutual. *Bottomly, huh? Sounds downright British. A Brit who hates the Irish maybe? Was that why he's so hard set that I'm guilty? Could prejudice be driving this bloke's vendetta?* It was something to consider.

Scraping his thumbnail over the fine filigree inked on the business card, a whisper niggled at the back of Ash's mind. Something he could nah put his finger on, but something important. Something he should have done, as if he'd missed an important date or forgotten a customer order. As if he'd left his stove on. Puzzled, he flipped the card over, then flipped it to its fine front again. *Leviathan Mutual.* Why did that name sound familiar?

The bloke's phone rang until it call-forwarded Ash to another number, then dialed it for him. He sat waiting, his gut in knots along with every muscle in his body. At last. A voice answered. Ash blinked, not believing what—or who—he heard on the other end of that line. "Hammer? Is that you?"

"Ah, sorry. Wrong num—"

"Hammer!" Ash jumped to his feet. "Don't you be hanging up on me! I know 'tis you. What the bloody hell?"

But click. The line went dead.

"Hammer answered?" Kevin asked, his voice filled with disbelief.

Ash stared at the phone in his hand. "Aye. 'Twas Hammer." *Me friend?*

Surrender was not the Ranger way. Neither was giving up when the going got tough, by hell. Colby grunted, putting everything into escaping the plastic ties that hindered the circulation in her arms and shoulders. She had to do this quickly, yet passively. Losing her head would only waste time and energy she couldn't spare. Who knew how long she'd be stuck down here?

You can do this, because you've done it before. Damn straight.

She'd practiced this exact scenario in the Army, only this time, her wrists were bound together over a lead pipe. Without knowing where the door to this small room was, or if there was one—she could've been dropped in through a hole in the ceiling—Colby settled cross-legged to work her escape.

It's not a matter of if, but when...

Whoever'd fastened the zip-ties must've been a novice. They were loose. Not only loose, but wrist-to-wrist restraints made for easier escapes. A professional would never have been this sloppy.

One point in her favor. Whoever kidnapped her was no career criminal.

She'd already shimmied the ratcheting tail of the tie until it faced her. Then she clamped it between her teeth and pulled to make sure it was snug, good and tight until it hurt to the point of cutting her skin.

Ready? Oh, hell yeah.

Sucking in a cleansing breath, Colby lifted to her knees and stretched both arms forward as far as she could extend them. Then, with the pipe against her cheek, she pulled back, jerked both elbows down, and... *SNAP!*

Okay, that hurt, and she was certain both wrists were bleeding, but she was free. "In your face!" she spat into the dark, rubbing her sore arms to promote circulation. Not like being free solved everything, but now she was pissed and dangerous, too.

"I'm coming for you," she called to whoever was on the other side of her ceiling. "So run, you chicken shit coward! Run while you still can!"

CHAPTER TWENTY-FOUR

Even the cool breeze on the street offered no air. No oxygen. Ash couldn't think. His mind wouldn't clear. Out of patience, he signaled the valet to bring Hammer's Lexus around again. They knew him by sight, he'd called for the car enough.

There'd been no word from Colby and none from BPD. It was as if she'd disappeared in the same thin air he now fought to catch a breath in. Ash knew it might be futile, but he was intent on a face-to-face with his buddy. Whatever Hammer Dugan was up to, it had something to do with the

Beantown arsonist, Colby, and maybe Liam too, though how, Ash had no idea.

He hit the gas the moment he cleared the rounded drive at the hotel entrance. Left at the corner, he aimed for Hammer's quaint little bungalow up north in Cambridge. It took minutes to make the distance, and by then, he verged on losing his slim hold on his control.

The bloody bugger hung up on me. You don't do that to your friends. You just don't.

The car moved as predicted in its commercials, gliding easily around the curves and hugging the corners that led to Hammer's residence, a red brick Colonial built back from the street on a half-acre filled with trees and shrubs. Similar homes completed the prestigious cul-de-sac, all with two-car garages and primly landscaped lawns.

For a struggling insurance salesman with a wife who didn't work and three kids under the age of five, Hammer certainly lived the life. Bold black shutters attended each of the eight second-level casement windows. Picture windows adorned the lower level, their sills underscored by empty flower boxes. But 'twas the fine grand entryway that brought a surge of bile to the back of Ash's throat, forcing the need to spit. Bloody hell, you would have thought General George Washington hisself lived here instead of a simple, lowly insurance salesman.

Two cream-white columns abutted the five wide concrete stairs, themselves protected beneath a grand portico painted the same color. For a colonial, the place had enough ginger-breading at each corner and edge to make it look—odd—in a pathetic, after-thought sort of way. The canvas-covered sailboat parked on the concrete pad aside the garage, its naked mast pointed skyward, added to the unsettled aura of the home.

The day turned dismal with rain, matching Ash's flagging spirit. He'd dialed Colby's phone enough to know her battery was dead by now. Or that someone had removed it.

Parking across the street, before the cul-de-sac circled in on itself, Ash left the Lexus behind. He palmed his phone and brought up the app for a swift ride home. One way or the other, he had no more use for his supposed friend's car. Not unless Hammer had a good reason for ditching his call. Ash would love to hear it.

Taking two steps at a time, he rang Hammer's bell and waited while the drizzle increased to a downpour. Thunder rumbled, and Ash ran a hand over the back of his neck, needing to hit someone.

After another round of knuckles to the wood, his angst ramped beyond the need to know where Hammer was and into pure aggravation. Ash didn't have time for one more dead end in this gods' blessed day. Where the hell was Hammer or his wife? Was she too sick she could nah tend to the bell? If she was, where was Hammer? Why was he not here to care for her? Where were their children? It made no sense.

For good measure, Ash took a tour around the house and into the backyard. No toys anywhere. No picnic table. No swing set in the shade. Nothing indicated that a family with wee children lived here. What the bloody hell was going on?

Tired of the chase, he called up his friends on Uber. He had better things to do than wait on a jerk with no loyalty. Damn Hammer to hell.

"Hello?"

A voice! Roused out of her exhausted stupor at the first sign of life above her, Colby pressed both palms to what she now knew was a floor instead of a ceiling and called out as loudly as her sore throat would allow, "I'm here! Down here!"

"For pity sake, who's beneath my floor?" Same female voice. Dumb question.

Probably because you put me here? A whopping dose of suspicion came along with the tiny wisp of hope unfurling in Colby's chest. How had this person heard her when no one else could? What alerted this supposed rescuer to call out when Colby's voice had long since turned hoarse and raspy from yelling into the cold. No one had heard her these last few hours. Why had this woman? Tired of the futility in screaming for help, she'd resigned herself to a long, dark, lonely night of fighting off rats and spiders, if it truly was night. Colby couldn't tell. Stashed within the foundation of some building that could be anywhere, she certainly wasn't in plain sight. Still..

"Can you get me out of here? P-please?" she asked raggedly. Her lips were dry, her butt was sore from sitting on concrete, and if that rat—or rats— came back one more time, she might have to kill and eat them. Not that she wouldn't, but ewwwww. The thought of bloody, squirming rat flesh in her bare hands repulsed Colby to her deepest core, but by hell, survive she would.

"Umm, maybe," the woman overhead replied. "Let me see what I can do. I'll try. Don't go anywhere."

Don't go anywhere? My God, I'm being saved by an idiot who thinks I'm as dumb as she is. But, oh well. Out of this basement hole, if that's what this dank prison cell was, would still be better than sitting her shivering.

Colby scrambled to her knees, now stiff from her cramped confinement. Her rat friend had continued making quick visits, but not once had he set his sticky toes on her bare skin again. Still, she could hear him. His squeaks and pitter-patters were not those of a tiny mouse. And more than once, she'd felt a snakelike tail by her ankle. She pegged him at maybe the size of a small cat. Or dog. Or—*my hell, get me out of here!*

Too angry at having been ambushed and chilled by the change in weather to sit still, she'd handled every square inch of her six-foot by eight-foot tomb-like prison, searching for any way to escape and also to keep warm. She'd found nothing but floorboards and wooden joists overhead, concrete walls lined with jagged rebar spikes on all four sides.

The floor was dirt and the air had gotten steadily colder, which meant night had fallen or Boston was in for one of its legendary spring storms. This dark place reminded her of the horrors endured by American prisoners of war in Vietnam. Those poor men had been stuffed into cages and concrete boxes, too.

Colby wanted out despite the sure knowledge that the person *rescuing* her was likely who'd abducted her. No matter. This timid voice was the first to acknowledge she still lived. Colby intended to keep on living.

Scraping and thumping sounded overhead. Then something heavy being dragged or pushed. At any rate, it scraped loudly enough Colby could follow its path above the traffic noises. Dirt and dust trickled over her head, but anything was endurable now.

At last, a light cracked Colby's ceiling as floorboards were lifted, one by one, then set aside. There was no trapdoor, which explained why she'd found no clasp or lever from below. Whoever'd stashed her had simply taken up part of the floor to hide her.

A shiver slithered across her shoulders. How many concrete pits were there in this nightmare? Could there be more women stuck in here? *Then I'll just have to rescue them after I'm out of here. Once I call Ash. And the police. And my mom.*

At last enough floorboards were cleared out of her way. Colby angled her shoulders up and through the four-by-eight joists. Thankful, but cautious, she palmed the beam and hefted the rest of herself up and out of that dingy pit. Only after she was up on her feet again did she turn to face the crazy woman at her back, the one in the weird long skirt and cape.

She was a tiny thing with dark hair that hung in thick, *those-can't-be-real* sausage-like ringlets, and—you got it—a bonnet. She totally had the Dickens' look down, and she acted as timid. Except for her make-up.

That was more Mae West than kindly Bob Cratchit's wife. Ruby red lips. Rounded cheeks pink with blush. A speck of a mole above her upper lip. Blinking, Mae West cocked her head as if she didn't know what to make of the woman who'd just climbed out of her floor.

Then how'd you know to loosen those precise floorboards, huh? You liar.

Colby knew better but decided to play along until she could make a break for cover. Dusting her palms to her thighs, she dared her would-be rescuer to spin another lie.

"How'd you find me?" she asked, her voice so hoarse she had to project just to be heard. But the effort made her sound innocent, too. As if she believed her good fortune at being *saved.* Yeah, not so much. But she could act too, damn it.

"You must be thirsty," her rescuer offered breathlessly instead of answering. Another doe-eyed blink had Colby wondering if the lights were on but no one was home inside that empty head. But what an innocent *sounding* voice this odd woman had, complete with an ultra-feminine quaver that had always made Colby want to up-chuck.

Why do women talk like that? As if they're weak and pitiful when they're not. Of course I'm thirsty! And you're stupid!

Frazzled, she latched onto the bottle of water extended from this dimwit damsel's hand, not surprised to see the woman's bright red fingernails were capped with black tips, another sign of crazy in Colby's book. Check.

"Thanks," she said evenly before she twisted the cap off and slugged down a good long swallow, keeping her eyes on Mae West. *Water. Wow.* You never know how good it feels going down until you've had to go without it.

While she swallowed, Colby too stock of her surroundings. The room beyond Mae West was strange. The three kerosene lamps on the floor cast a golden glow over a round woven rag rug that lay across an empty wooden chest that a man could've fit in if he were stupid enough to get inside. Colby wasn't. The thing looked like a crudely made coffin turned into a coffee table.

Shifting her bare feet, she tightened her right hand into a fist, offering the bulk of her left shoulder as her first line of defense, prepared to strike if Mae West so much as took one step in her direction. "Who are you?" She damned well needed to know. "And where am I?"

"Why I... I'm Delores." The woman's voice was as light as a dandelion puff on the wind, and twice as annoying. "And you're here." She waved at the hole in her floor. "How ever did you get down there?"

"You tell me," Colby shot back at her. "You put me there."

Mae West—Delores—whatever!—fluttered her fingertips against her high-button collar as if the notion made her faint of heart. "I would never." Blink, blink. Gasp, gasp. Lie, lie, lie.

Yeah, not buying the act, sister.

Colby backed away, not sure where she was headed, but damned sure on her way out of this looney bin. Traffic meant people, so that was here she'd run. She had to be in a town somewhere.

Maybe Boston. There'd be time to interrogate Delores later.

Get your ass out of here, Quaid. Move it!

She made it as far as the door, when it opened, damned near knocking her over. The last thing she saw was a fist coming at her, then—*BLAM!*

Somewhere on her way down to the floor, she heard that idiot woman behind her singing, *"Ring around the rosie. Pockets full of posies. Ashes, ashes, we all fall... dowwwwwwwwwn."*

CHAPTER TWENTY-FIVE

Bloody hell! The news wasn't good. According to Kev, the FBI was now involved and in transit to the hotel. They wanted Ash and everyone else on-site when they showed, but Ash had every reason to believe this new development had more to do with him being Liam's brother, and nothing with finding Colby. Desperate and going out of his feckin' mind, he ignored the federal summons, left the hotel, and caught a cab to Beacon Hill.

The nagging presence of Leviathan Mutual went with him. He had yet to make contact with their brutal investigator, but Ash knew now why the name bugged him. Hammer worked for Leviathan Mutual. Coincidence? *Nah by all the bloody saints in heaven.*

Despite the pouring rain, Ash asked the cabbie to drop him at the west end of Boston Commons, so he could walk up Beacon Hill to see what he'd missed before. Colby's disappearance had to have something to do with yesterday morning's fire. But how, he didn't know. He couldn't draw a straight line through the evidence at his fire in Southie and get it to link up with Colby's home here on the Hill. Not unless he'd missed something...

Ash let his eyes wander as he set his long legs to the task while traffic maneuvered the narrow street, itself lined with parked cars and delivery trucks. The house on the far west corner was still under construction, plastic sheeting covering the front facing, with sawhorses set to barricade the newly poured concrete walk. Ah, but rich folk were the same the world over. They already had it all, and yet they wanted more. What this grand old home needed was a cover of ivy and roses, not more concrete.

Tourist buses rumbled past him in the rain, leaving silvery gray puffs of diesel fumes in their misty wakes. Bikers. Walkers. Despite the weather, people were everywhere, even mothers in revealing spandex outfits who ran by pushing racing baby-strollers, splashing through puddles in some crazed need to keep their already lithe bodies fit. What were they thinking, looking the way they did while tending their wee children? America was a lusty, beautiful—but daft—land.

At last at Bella's front door and drenched to the skin, Ash climbed the steps. It looked like some onerous bloke had already cut the police tape, its broken pieces now fluttering in the chilly breeze. He went inside and shut the door behind him.

Stopping there, he took in every last detail of the grand entry. Bella's fine home was an example of how early America had squandered its remarkable wood resources, as if the great pine and oak forests were an unlimited resource. Just like Ireland and every other civilized country before them. *God, be merciful on us all.*

Each doorway had been framed with thick white pine, the walls topped off with lavish crown molding. Each step up the magnificent winding staircase was solid oak, the likes you couldn't buy today unless you were rich. But none of the wood was polished and proud. Even the American eagle over the double entry didn't glow as it should.

Ah, if Ash lived here, if he ever owned a home this palatial, he'd refinish every bit of the wooden floor, and he'd polish every banister and balustrade until the whole place gleamed like the treasure it was. But—he swallowed hard over the sudden lump in his throat. This was not his home, and because of him, Colby was missing.

Standing here in her home but without her in his arms gave a man pause, was what it did. Fighting the futility of the day, Ash's spirit lagged for the first time. There were no leads. Nothing solid to go on. No ransom call and no way to know if this was even a kidnapping. Bella's nonsensical ramblings meant nothing. A blue-eyed woman? Blimey, how many of them were in Boston? Running around in a cape? That may narrow the playing field, but—

Mary, Joseph, and Jesus! What if I never see Colby's pretty face again?

Bowing his chin to his weary chest, Ash needed to be sure and strong before he dared look Colby's poor mother in the eye again. How could he tell Bella that he couldn't find Colby?

It was then he spied the slender print of a woman's bare foot in the sooty grime at his feet.

Saints be praised. He took a knee, peering down at what might be his first clue. Colby had been here, he was sure of it. That was her wee print. Didn't that fire up the pistons in his worried heart? Carefully, so as not to disturb what he now believed was more than just an arson crime scene, maybe one of abduction as well, he turned a full circle. Her shoes. Praise the Lord, her running shoes were both stashed back beside the front door.

"Colby?" he rang out, daring to hope. "Are you in here?"

It was worth a try, but he knew better than to expect an answer. No. She wouldn't have gone willingly without her shoes.

Tugging his cell phone from his front trouser pocket, he began gathering evidence. Photo after photo, he concentrated on the path he'd tromped over, willing his eyes to truly see the story Colby had unknowingly left for him. Another bare footprint faced his way from the doorway, then the one he'd first spied. Okay, so she'd come into the house, but why leave her shoes behind? It made no sense. There wasn't a single print beyond that. No sign she'd gone farther. Only her running shoes, tossed near the door as if they were no longer needed.

But wait. Ash crouched to the floor again, holding his breath. At a right angle to Colby's bare footprint—another print. Not the rubber-soled print that a fireman's boot might've left, but the slick, smooth sole of a dress shoe. Bloody hell, a gent's shoe.

A crushing blow to the heart, damn it! Liam never wore anything but the finest leather shoes. He truly was in Boston then, and he'd come to exact his vengeance on his little brother, the dastardly scoundrel.

Ash thumb dialed Bella's hotel room, his heart beating like a banshee. At first ring, he barked, "Kevin. Get me Kevin."

"He's a little busy at the moment. The FBI's here. Where are you?" Tula asked pointedly, right before she answered herself with, "You're hiding!"

Her and her bloody questions and answers. Ash balked. Did he dare tell her or the FBI? Could he trust that arm of the federal government to help him find Colby, or would they throw up roadblocks to hinder his every step because of his ties to Liam O'Callaghan?

"You're not going to answer, are you?" Tula hushed as if she'd cupped a hand over the phone.

"I can nah," he admitted before she answered

that, too, "but tell Kevin I'm sending him photos I just took inside Bella's home. Someone's been here, a man in fine shoes, and I found traces of Colby as well. I'm certain 'tis her tiny footprint I'm looking at. I need Kevin to get these pictures to his arson investigator. I need to know if he agrees with me."

"Praise the Lord," Tula whispered. "Find her, Ash. You bring our baby girl home."

"I will," he promised with all his Irish heart. "But don't tell Bella. Not yet. Don't get her hopes up." *Like mine.*

His throat dry at this new development, and at the very real prospect that he might soon be wanted for questioning by the FBI, Ash disconnected with Tula and backtracked, careful not to step where he hadn't already put his big feet.

Ah, the tender scene. Colby's sweet bare foot alongside the tread of his giant boot print. It nearly broke his heart to leave even this small part of her behind.

Opening the front door, Ash peered up and down the street before he set one foot to the step. Nothing had changed. 'Twas still raining. Bostonians, more of them protected with umbrellas now, carried on with their lives as if no one was missing in their fair city. As if everything were fine and perfect. What he wouldn't give for that to be so.

With a hand still on Bella's lavishly detailed wrought iron railing, Ash stopped in his tracks. There. Three doors down. A woman hurried through the misty rain. He could only see the back of her long skirt and bonnet because they were hidden beneath a dark blue cape.

Sweet Baby Jesus, could Bella be right after all?

Warmer now that she was in a room that was not in the cellar, Colby could barely lift her head. Drool or blood, probably both, dripped over her bottom lip. The ropes at her wrists and across her chest and waist were harsh and tight, but her feet and legs were free. Bound to a heavy wooden chair, her captors had allowed little slack for her to breathe.

Escape, it seemed, was futile this time. What a waste to have survived the gauntlet of a Ranger's life only to end up a powerless victim. Damn. This made twice in one day—at least Colby hoped it was the same day—that she'd been blindsided, most likely by the same sneaky asshole who'd stuffed her into that basement pit in the first place.

There were at least two people in the murky darkness around her, one spineless husband and the one crazy female in the cape, who sniped back at him for him not being the man she thought she'd married. Mae West—for lack of being able to remember the crazy woman's real name— seemed in charge, though how that worked, Colby had no idea. Mae was not the sharpest blade in the drawer. Whatever she had under her long skirt had to be some powerful aphrodisiac to make a man twice her size kidnap another woman for her.

Colby was a realist. She knew where this nightmare was headed. Given the place where her search for Bella had ended, at her family home on Beacon Hill, she now realized her mother's disappearance had been a ploy to get at her. And it made sense. Colby had certainly pissed off enough people over the years, disgruntled cheerleaders, unsatisfied boyfriends, losing soccer opponents, maybe even a few fellow soldiers who thought she'd owed them something. Any one of them might have cracked up and come after her. Hell, that scenario also explained Ash's run-in with the Beantown Stalker. The arsonist wasn't Liam after all.

Uh-uh. The arsonist was these two nut jobs. They were also behind Bella's disappearance. Colby just had to figure out how she knew them. She had to get them to talk and tell her where Bella was. If only she could.

Lolling her heavy head to the side, Colby chuckled in a sick, thick way. Blood clots in a person's throat and mouth tended to make laughing out loud difficult. So did the gag in her mouth. But worse was the throbbing pain in her head and the quivering sensation at the back of her throat that signaled her need to throw up. The human skull was not made to withstand much brute force and two hard knocks in one day made concussion a very real possibility.

But these people were a joke. If Colby hadn't been so focused on finding Bell this morning, the bland-looking guy nodding at the woman like a cowed dog would never have gotten the best of her. He just wasn't man enough. Medium build. Medium brown thinning hair. The guy even wore a nondescript, medium brown suit over a rumpled light tan dress shirt. That was all he was, medium bland oatmeal on two legs.

But damn him. Whoever he was, he'd been

waiting just inside her front door for her. By the rank, sweaty smell of him, he'd been there all night, probably scared to return empty-handed the way Mae West continually sniped at him. The way he had yet to stand up for himself and talk back, even once. But he had most definitely hit Colby the moment she'd cleared the doorway. What a rookie, FNG mistake, to dash into home territory thinking it was safe just because it was home. Yeah, not smart.

"She's awake," the female of this wacked-out duo sputtered, suddenly all breathy and femme fatale-ish sounding again.

"Yeah," Colby choked. "I'm awake," she meant to say. It came out more like "Ah um make," through the gag.

"Why'd you hit her so hard?" Same dumb chick. Different dumb question.

"I already told you. You weren't supposed to let her out, and I wasn't expecting to see her when I opened the door. I didn't mean to, she was just there and I freaked."

Yeah. A five-foot tall, barefoot woman in a t-shirt is scary like that.

"So, call him," Crazy lady demanded. Make that Crazy Me West.

"*You* call him. He's already mad at me. 'Sides, he knows my voice." *Big wuss.*

A feminine growl. "Fine then. Give me your phone. Jiminy crickets, I have to do everything."

Jiminy Crickets? Really? Haven't heard that since grade school.

Colby held her breath, which was not hard to do since she could barely draw in a deep breath any way. But then everything got worse. With a glug, glug, glug, the rancid fumes of diesel fuel hit Colby's nostrils. Turning her nose into her shoulder, she choked as her situation disintegrated into a hellish nightmare. Time was definitely running out.

Big Wuss splashed the fuel around the room but thank God! He hadn't poured any on her. Not like it mattered. The fumes were enough to turn this old house into the biggest fireball Boston would ever see. She wouldn't live through it, but still. Not wearing diesel fuel was a tiny silver lining in a very dark place.

"Is this Mister Ash Callahan?" Mae West asked.

Colby's head jerked up. *She's calling Ash?*

"Shut up and listen. You'd better come down to..." The bitch had marbles in her lying mouth. Colby couldn't make out the address, not the way the woman switched into some perverted Irish accent at the last minute with a bright, "We'll be waitin'. Good day to ya, sir!"

"No," Colby ground out. She'd changed her mind. This wasn't about her or Bella. These monsters had to be Liam and his woman. Ash needed to stay the fuck away. They'd kill him for sure!

CHAPTER TWENTY-SIX

"Aye, but I'm already here," Ash purred as he stepped around the corner and into view. He'd followed the shocked lady—and he used the term loosely—when she'd pranced into the home on the northwest corner like she'd owned the place. Up she'd gone, three stories u, to the first bedroom on the right.

But Ash had done his homework before he'd set one boot to the narrow staircase that led him here. The pungent smell of diesel fuel in the air confirmed his suspicions. 'Twas diesel Liam had used to burn his childhood home after he'd killed his parents. And now he'd come to America to finish the job. *Nah bloody likely.*

Liam was no small problem. Twice as muscular as Ash, he'd boxed as a youth, no doubt when he'd gotten his lust for blood and brutal violence. That alone demanded Ash quell the impulse to charge that woman and choke her spitless until she talked and told him where Colby was. Whatever happened next had to be handled with finesse. There could be no gunplay or match. No metal striking against metal. Diesel wouldn't allow it. Neither would Liam.

Of all the times to wonder if Colby—if she were even in this building—still carried that slim little blade, the one he called her ankle-biter. She'd better not use it if she did. One flick of that blade might send this elegant fixer-upper to the moon. There'd been no time to alert Kevin, simply because Ash didn't want the FBI barging in, guns blazing. He'd watched the news. He knew how heavy-handed they could be. *Not. This. Time.*

The little thing in the cape with her ear to the phone whirled on him like a cat with its claws already out and spitting. "How'd you get here so fast?" Her eyes widened. "You followed me!"

She thought she had the right to be indignant?

Was she daft?

Ash peered past her defiance into the dimly lit room, searching for sight of Colby or an accomplice. He had no doubt he could take this little lady, but he was quite sure she wasn't acting on her own. No. It was Liam he needed to see. Liam, he meant to kill—after he saved Colby. *Where is she?*

Before he'd followed the woman inside, Ash checked the perimeter of the house. There was no electricity, its power line disrupted by the owner's need for that fancy sidewalk out front. Two kerosene lamps now sat on the floor at her feet, but neither was lit. Still, Colby was in this house somewhere. She had to be.

He called out to her. "Colby? Can you hear me, Lass?"

Urgent mumbling from behind the daft woman met his ear, inciting a ruby red rage at his peripheral. That sound had to be from Colby. *I knew it. She's here somewhere. If they've hurt her...*

The lady in the cape flounced a step closer, blocking his view of the room, but she couldn't block the growls from Colby Quaid.

She's alive, but she must be restrained. Or she'd be swearing a blue streak and kicking this chit's ass.

Ash needed to get to Colby. Odds were slim

there'd be survivors once this caped woman lit the diesel. Banking on the sure knowledge that bullies of the world were too cowardly to risk their own lives, Ash took another step into the room.

"Stay where you are," the skirt ordered, her eyes flashing.

Ash took a better look at her. Gaudy make-up. Perhaps she was an extra for some show in town? He couldn't decide. "You grow that wart by yourself?" he taunted her ladyship.

She tossed her head, causing a cascading effect of tangles and spirals to spill over her cape. Her crafty fingers, no doubt holding a detonator or a lighter, might be obscured in the folds of her skirt. But where he'd expected a pithy comeback, he got sauce instead. The shrew giggled, then lifted both shoulders in what she probably thought was—cute.

"Where's me brother?" he asked, tired of the game, and Colby's time running out. To the darkness in the room, he bellowed, "Show yourself, Liam! For once in your bloody life, step out of the shadows and be a man."

Didn't he get the surprise of his life? 'Twas not Liam who stepped around the skirt. 'Twas—

"Hammer?" Ash had to ask, not believing what

he was seeing. "What are you doing here?"

But the dominos were already falling inside his head. The insurance policy he hadn't signed. Hammer's pushy insistence that he sign. The rounds and rounds of drinking, all on Hammer's tab. The backslapping. The sales pitch that wouldn't end until Ash walked out of Shenanigan Rose because Hammer wouldn't take no for an answer. The attack-dog investigator from Leviathan Mutual. Why was he convinced Ash torched his own place? *Because of the lies Hammer told him.*

The woman giggled, swishing her skirts back and forth like a spoiled little girl who'd just gotten a pony for her birthday. "Told you he'd be surprised."

Hammer didn't look surprised. He looked— caught. Sweat gleamed off his bottom lip. He blinked rapidly now he'd been forced to step into view. "It wasn't supposed to go down like this, mate."

"*Mate?*" Ash asked, his index finger pointed to his sternum. "Is this how you treat your *mate?* Your brother? You kidnap his woman and you set fire to his livelihood? You set him up to take the fall for what? Why?"

"Oh, pish posh," the skirt tossed back at Ash as

if this were a parlor game. "That old place of yours went up like" —she lifted one hand over her head and snapped her fingers— "toast!" Just that fast, she sang, "Ashes, ashes. We all fall down!"

Her squeal at the end of her idiotic song riled Ash. Already seeing red, he lashed out at Hammer. "Who the bloody hell is she?"

"M-my wife." Hammer blinked as if stunned that Ash didn't know. "Delores. I thought I'd introduced her before. Surely you've met."

Ash shook his head, disgusted. His fists clenched to knock Hammer's bugger of a *mate* into the harbor and him with her. "I do nah understand. You loaned me your car. Why? Did you bug it or..." *He wouldn't dare!* "Did you put one of those GPS tracker things in it? Have you been spying on me?"

Hammer shook his head so hard the sparse hairs on his head bobbed. "I wouldn't do that to you. I loaned you my car just to be nice."

Ash dug his hand over his head. "Nice! You call all this feckin' nice?"

"Just leave," Hammer urged, his shaky hands forward, as if placating an impossible situation. "Go now. You don't need to see this. It'll just hurt your feelings, and—"

As if burning Colby to death behind his back wouldn't hurt his bloody feelings? "I'll nah leave without her. Colby!" Ash roared. "Where is she? What have you done to her, you feckin' sot?"

The psychotic bitch at Hammer's side rolled her eyes and her haughty head rolled with them. "Shut up, Callahan. Your little girlfriend's right here." Stepping aside, she waved him into the room. "See? She's right here where you can't get to her."

Ash finally saw Colby, tied to a chair in the farthest corner with streaks of dark blood on her face and down the front of her t-shirt. Two desperate eyes gleamed back at him, but the poor thing was gagged. She jerked forward, but the chair they had her tied to didn't move.

His vision dimmed red with rage. "Let her go or so help me—"

"So help you what?" Delores sneered. "This is all your fault you know, *Mr. Callahan.*" Sarcasm ripped out of her. "Hammer tried to tell you what would happen if your place burned down, but did you listen? Even once? Oh, no..." She swiveled her hips, taunting him. "The mighty Scot always knows best. All the time and money my boy wasted trying to get you to buy—"

"He's Irish, Delores," Hammer murmured out

of the corner of his mouth, his eyes glued to Ash.

"He's what?" Her brows clashed together like two pieces of a very scary puzzle.

"He's from Ireland. He's Irish, not Scottish."

"I don't care if he's from the moon! It's still his fault," Delores screeched as she stabbed her index finger at Ash. "If he'd been a smarter Irishman and signed with you like you told him, none of this would've happened. You'd have gotten a fine commission, and I'd have my *baby!*" She took a menacing step in Ash's direction, still bellowing. "It's all your fault!"

Hammer cast an exasperated, sad look at his wife.

"Is that what these fires are about? Me nah signing an insurance policy? Nah signing with you?" Ash growled at Hammer, puzzled that these two fools thought torching his business and killing Colby could ever change his mind. What the bloody hell were they smoking?

"Not really." Hammer shook his head in the sneaky way of a weak man who didn't want his wife to catch him.

Jesus, Mary, and Joseph! Ash's eyes finally opened. "'Twasn't you, was it? Ye're nah the one who started the fires." He turned to Delores.

"'Twas you!"

She curtsied, that same blood-red fingernail now stabbed to her chin. "It's been me all along, you big dumb ox." Again with the hip swish of her skirts. "I'm the clever one, huh?"

Ash turned on his traitorous friend. "And what are you, her feckin' protector?" Not bloody likely. The man had no balls!

Another furtive glance at his wife, and Hammer lived down to Ash's expectations. He ducked his head into his shoulders like a guilty boy whose testicles had yet to drop. But Delores couldn't have carried Colby up three flights of stairs. Hammer was up to his neck in this daft scheme. He'd known how crazy she was since the first fire on the dock. Since the first shipping container. Because he'd been there with her.

"What'd you do? Buy the petrol for her and put it where she told you to like a good little boy?" Ash bit out, ready to knock this jerk on his ass. "Did you stay long enough to watch me place burn? Did you see me...?" He refused that last word. Never would he admit to shedding one tear to this liar.

Hammer's shamed gaze hit the floor at his feet, but proud Delores pitched her neck forward and whined, "What'd you expect? I can't carry those heavy cans by myself."

It all made sense now. Hammer was the brawn, she the twisted brains behind the arsons. "You told her everything about me. The types of woods I use. Me hours. Me orders. You forged illegal orders. I could've gone to prison!"

"If you'd lived." The witch had the nerve to shrug. "I was pretty upset with you."

Upset! How can a mother simply be... God, no! Ash couldn't bear the thought. "Where are your wee ones? Your children?" There'd been none at Hammer's home in Cambridge. "What have you done with them?" *Did you burn them, too?*

"What do you care?" Her hands fell to the folds in her skirt. "I can't buy another now, can I?"

Ye gods, the woman was as daft as the robins that ate fermented plums on his da's farm in spring. Children were not bought and sold like things. They were treasured. Loved. Not possessed!

"I trusted you," Ash told his lying friend, "and you used me. You set me up."

Delores lifted her palms out from her skirt and raised them to the ceiling with a demented sing-songy rendition of, "Ring around the rosie. Pockets full of posies. Ashes. Ashes. You'll both fall down!"

CHAPTER TWENTY-SEVEN

Try as she might, Colby couldn't budge this damned chair. Not an inch! Ash had to leave, now! *Get out of here!* These two were playing him. She hadn't known who the guy was until Ash named him, but Hammer had concealed a knife in the sheath in the back of his pants. Delores had a lighter hidden in her skirt pocket. No one would walk out of here alive.

Colby signaled him around the dirty rag in her mouth, and he nodded knowingly, but no one could translate "Mgh muh!" into "Get out! Save yourself!"

Desperate now, she threw her weight forward, growling with every beat of her heart, needing Ash to forsake her before they both went up in flames. Damn him! Inch by inch, he edged sideways, risking all to get around Delores. Did he not understand?

Kicking at the ropes that held her, Colby shook her head in frustration, tears spilling over her cheeks, begging Ash to save himself. *Listen to me, damn it! Hear what I cannot tell you!* Her time was gone, and if he didn't leave this very minute, his would be, too. *'Leave me behind,'* she prayed. *'You're the dreamer. Go dream! Fly! Just live. Goddamn it, Ash. Live!*

As if he'd heard, Ash speared her with a look— *that look*—the one that clearly told her he meant to die for her. But then he winked and blew her a tiny kiss, the cavalier Irish fool!

No. No. No! Don't do anything stupid! I love you too much to let you die! I'm not worth it!

Of course, Mad Hatter's head swiveled on top of her skinny neck to watch Colby unravel. Delores cocked a devilish grin, obviously enjoying the pain and humiliation she'd caused—right before the sharpened point of a wooden stake pierced the ruffles of her cape. Instead of smiling, she chirped an odd little squeak, then burped a rivulet of blood.

"No!" Hammer screamed at the sight. "Not my Delly! You killed her!"

"Aye," Ash growled, another stake fisted in his hand. With one sideways stoke, he slammed it home, stabbing the man through the chest. Hammer fell alongside his insane wife, both staked through the heart like a couple vampires.

Colby blinked at the force of that hit, the kickback of blood and tissue splattered into the wall behind Hammer. Her gaze flittered instantly to Ash. Her hero. Her savior. *Who are you?*

Ash flew to her, his long fingers sure and apparently quite lethal as he loosened the gag. Just as quickly, the tangled ropes pooled at her feet.

"Ash," she cried the second the gag dropped. She would've flung herself into his arms if he hadn't scooped her against the wild beat of his heart. Deftly she wrapped her arms around his poor burned neck and cried, "Let's get out of here."

"Do nah let me go," he ordered. As if she could or ever would. "This bloody place is going to blow."

Her knight in shining armor dashed out the door and thundered down the dark stairs. They didn't get far.

No sooner had they cleared the last step when the entry door pushed inward, bringing Ash up short. He reared back, his shoulder turned, shielding Colby from whoever was on their way in. But a Ranger had to know who was on the battlefield. She craned her neck to see around Ash's thick bicep. "Liam? Is that you?"

"Aye. 'Tis him," Ash confirmed with a throaty growl. "In all his filthy glory." *Could the day get any feckin' worse?*

Liam grunted, his shoulders as wide as ever, the sneer on his ugly mug as thick with disdain as the last time Ash had dealt with him. "Christ man, is that all ye have to say to your long lost brother?"

"I'll nah be offering you asylum if that's why ye're here. Nor money. So leave."

As if things could go down that easily. Liam was a big man, practiced in the wicked ways of the world. The only reason Ash had survived his last fisticuffs with the man was the siren of a passing police car. The O'Callaghan farmhouse had still smoldered that day. Already a wanted man, Liam had run and left unfinished business.

The bastard's eyes went dark as he scanned Colby from head to toe. When they lit on her chest, he grinned with disgusting approval that made Ash want to wretch. "This the chit you've been tupping? Nah the good little boy Mum thought you were, eh?"

Colby pressed herself into Ash's side, a feminine response he didn't expect, but one that bolstered his protective instincts. 'Twas Liam who'd once brazenly declared the size of a man's balls were all that kept his knees from knocking together like a woman's. Ash planted his feet wide, his declaration of war openly declared. *Take a good look, brother. I'm all grown up, and I'll kill you before you lay a hand on me woman.*

"Let me pass," he spat to the only other O'Callaghan alive on his branch of the family tree.

Liam canted his head, his long dark locks falling over his shifty, blue eyes. One pointed brow spiked in wry amusement as he lifted a micro butane torch into view and aimed it at Ash like a gun. "Din'nt you care why I'm here, little brother? Nor why I travelled all the way to America just to see the likes of you? Why I've been following you for days?"

Like Ash didn't already know that Liam was here to kill him. He'd vowed to end Ash the same way he'd ended their parents, but fire and blood. Why play fox-and-goose with the ass?

"I do nah care why ye're here. Let me pass." He kept Colby tucked into his side, but his throat was dry. She'd since wiggled to her feet, but he would not risk Liam getting his dirty hands on her.

Liam kicked the door shut behind him, drawing in a deep breath of the toxic petrol-laden air, his barrel chest stretching his fisherman sweater. "Ah," he gasped as if relishing the foul vapor, humping his sternum with one palm, the torch still in his other. "Smells just like home, does it nah? Just the way I remember before it burnt to the ground."

"You killed them!" Ash spat, not needing to be reminded of the horror of that day. Of the loss. "Mum and Da suffered, and you did it!"

Colby's gasp at his side lifted every tiny hair up the back of his neck, but yes. That was another truth he hadn't had the heart to tell her, not after the lovely consummation of their love. How could he have? She'd been glowing. 'Twas not the time nor the place to dash the golden light in her eyes with the awful tragedy of how his parents had burned to death by Liam's hand. How their eldest son had murdered them!

"I'll nah ask you again," Ash bit out, one foot shifted forward, balancing his weight to strike first. "Do nah think for one second I'll nah protect what's mine."

Liam took a wide stance as well, forever challenging those he deemed weaker, which was everyone. The bloody fool. "Did Da nah teach you anything? You'll stay 'til I tell you to go, little brother."

"If it's a fight you want," Ash growled, his fists already clenched, "at least let me set me woman aside, so she'll nah have to witness your ugly death." He meant to tell Colby to run for her life, and he prayed for once she'd listen.

"By all means," Liam sneered. "But do keep her close so I can finish her once I'm through with you. 'Tis time she knows what a real man feels like inside her bonnie body." He grabbed his crotch in a vulgar gesture, thrusting into his free hand as he might do with one of his ugly wenches. "I'm certain she'll appreciate the lesson by the time I'm through with her."

'I'll kill him,' Ash promised his mum and da even as he set Colby to the third step behind him. 'I'm sorry, but it has to be done. I cannah let him hurt any *more people, and he will nah—will nah!—hurt me woman the way he hurt you.'*

Damned if Colby wouldn't sit her ornery arse on that step, nor do as she was told. "Introduce me, Ash," she demanded, her voice oddly strained.

"No," Ash growled, keeping an eye on the murderer at his back. "Stay put. For once, stay out of this."

"For the love of Mike, introduce us," Liam bellowed. "Let me get to know the woman ye're about to lose. Who knows? I might decide to keep her if she's any good."

"No," Ash spat, but damn. Colby planted her palm in his chest, angling to get around him, not even sparing him a tender smile, which he very much needed. This fight would be his last, and he needed Colby far from it when it ended.

"Liam O'Callaghan, I presume?" she said hoarsely, her left hand stretched forward as if this were Easter morn, and they were merely on their way to Mass of the Resurrection at Boston's Cathedral of the Holy Cross. "I've heard so much about you!"

Gushing over Liam? Disobedient yet again? Gods, this woman!

Of course Liam's face split with a wicked,

salacious grin. What man's wouldn't? He had the bloody nerve to wink at Colby while he offered his hand, as if he had a right to touch her!

Jesus, Mary, and Joseph! Did she nah get the drift of this war between brothers? Did she nah understand how deeply Ash despised Liam? Apparently not. Ash wanted to tear his hair out when Colby dodged him, still reaching for his murderous brother. Like a friend!

Liam's cheek pinched with victory as he cast one last up-yours chin toss at Ash, but Colby didn't clasp his wide opened palm. Instead, she ducked in close and personal, past his big, ugly mitt as if going in for a womanly hug.

Bloody hell! Her mother's right. For two cents, I'll bend her over me knee and—

Ooomph.

"Bloody hell?" Liam choked as he lurched forward, his eyes gone as wide as saucers, while wee Colby stared up at him, all five feet nothing of her. Her left hand was spread flat on the right side of his chest as if she was holding him up. Like a big gentle giant who simply needed a hug, his hoary head curled onto her shoulder with pitiful groan.

Colby pressed her mouth to his ear and whispered, "Ash asked you nicely to leave, big brother O'Callaghan," she ground out, her fingers now clenched at the back of his thick neck. "You should've listened because he's the good guy in this marriage. He puts stars in the sky. I'm the one who makes sure assholes like you look up and see those fucking, beautiful creations he makes, got it?"

"Love, no," Ash bit out, not needing his woman to fight his battles for him. But marriage? Had she actually said the M word? And what was wrong with her voice?

Liam's butane torch clattered to the floor. He seemed to be having trouble breathing. Or moving. 'Twas then Ash caught sight of the blood spurting over Colby's other wrist, the one she held high in Liam's gut, right below his ribcage. *Holy Mother of God, she stabbed him.*

Ash nearly laughed at the sight, this wee woman bringing his bloodthirsty brother to heel. What was this rare magic she held?

Colby tossed a wink to Ash over her shoulder. "We're surrounded by losers, hon," she rasped. "Hammer and his bitch never found my knife. Apparently, Big Brother here wasn't expecting it, either."

"Always full of surprises, Lass," Ash said as he

stiff-armed the bloody murderer who'd stalked him for years. When he leaned Liam's back to the door behind him, the blade stuck in his gullet went with him. "I'm taking you outside, brother. 'Tisn't safe in here, nah with me woman pissed at you like she is. Don't think to run, though. You'll nah get far. She's a wee one, but she's also one of the first female Rangers in the United States Army, you know. Aye, she's fast, but I caught her."

"Shut yer feckin' pie-hole," Liam gasped, weaving, his bleary eyes cross-eyed as he tried to fix them on Colby. "Keep her... away from... me."

Ash tossed his cell phone to Colby. "Call the authorities, love. Tell 'em we've got Liam Callahan, the Beantown Stalkers, and" —ah, his Irish heart was smiling again— "you, Lass. I've finally got you."

CHAPTER TWENTY-EIGHT

Colby beamed so hard her cheeks hurt. By the time the FBI dragged Liam off in their very own ambulance, the county coroner was on scene. Three stories up. First bedroom to the right. Her right foot still twitched to march back up those stairs and kick Hammer's ass for knocking her out. Didn't matter that he was dead. He was a dick for getting the best of her—twice in one day!

The sun had set long ago. Kevin's boys had already cleared the home of petrol, then put down a layer of fire retardant foam to absorb the fumes, and, in the small chance of an accidental ignition, to squelch any flame before it caught its first breath of life.

The homeowners were on site and aghast that their lovely Victorian was now fodder for every news outlet on the East Coast. After a thorough search, the police concluded there were no other women to be saved, that the Dugan's had trapped only Colby beneath the floorboards once they'd broken into the place and taken advantage of the ongoing construction. The rain had stopped, and for now, Colby sat with Ash on the open tailgate of the first EMT wagon that had arrived on scene.

Her wrists had been treated and wrapped, and she was at peace. The knot on her head guaranteed her headache would last a couple days, but it wasn't enough reason for a ride to the emergency room. Bella was safe again with Tula, and the hotel had located Pierre in an adjoining room full of little children, who'd driven him crazy with affection. All in all, it was a very good end to the scary day.

Ash was in rare form, his name cleared and his spirits high. He'd demanded a warm blanket for Colby, when the medics finished checking her injuries, and he'd wrapped her up like a little girl, nearly turning her into a mummy. He had yet to remove his broad palm from the small of her back, though, where he'd tucked the tip of his finger into the waistband of her jeans, just enough to let her know they had unfinished business.

"Did I hear you in there? Did you say... marriage?" he asked. A delightful sparkle glinted in his blue eyes as he scratched his free hand over his head. The man was outrageously handsome, more so when he knew he was right.

Oh, that. Contentment giggled out of Colby as she kicked her bare feet. "I might have," she said quietly, since her sore throat had turned smoker husky. "Didn't you say that you protect what's yours?"

Her dashing Irishman winked, the tease. "Aye, I did. You din't need to stab me brother to prove you love me, though. What happened to your voice?"

"Nothing really. Just a sore throat from calling for help. But aye, you didn't have to stake those two vampires to prove you love me, either." She mimicked his accent as well as his cheeky smile.

"Don't go braggin', darlin'. You couldn't have gotten yourself out of this by yourself, nah this time. Nah with the likes of Bonnie and Clyde in there." His big chin nodded at the entry where poor Kevin stood with an army of Boston's finest at his beck and call.

Now that the Beantown Stalkers had been apprehended and their siege of the city was over, the mayor was on his way down for a press conference, a protocol nightmare of biblical proportions for the beleaguered fire chief.

"Admit it, you need me to protect you," Ash declared proudly and a little tenderly, hip bumping her.

Oh, that again. Him, Tarzan. Me might be Jane after all. "I *was* happy you showed up." She gave him that much. He'd never change, and Colby was okay with it. Now, if he'd just let her live it down.

Ash spread his hand at her back, warming and teasing as another finger slid past her waistband. "Marriage is a solemn vow between a man and his woman."

"It is," she agreed noncommittally, her belly clenching at the attention he suddenly commanded. "In some churches, I guess. Some religions."

"In some countries, 'tis the start of a week-long celebration."

"With your black beer and Irish whiskey, no doubt?"

"Aye," Ash said, his gaze deliberately dropping

to her mouth. "And more."

She licked her lips, wanting him to know she craved another taste of him. "Like?"

The world stilled as he leaned his forehead into hers. "Like handfasting and the sweet taste of honey mead toasts, Lass," he murmured, his voice thick and low, filled with that hot Irish brogue. "Like the bride's magic hankie and the trill of wedding bells from sun up to sun down. Like fairies and lucky days and luckier months and..."

Ash snapped his mouth shut as if he'd said too much, but his eyes kept talking. He didn't have to say a word. His love radiated straight from his heart to hers. She knew what was coming.

"Colby Quaid," he breathed, his voice rich with—trepidation? Anticipation? She couldn't decide. "I've never wanted anyone in me whole entire life as much as I want you. Will you...?" His throat flexed as he swallowed hard. "Will you walk with me?"

"A walk? Oh, sure." That she could certainly do. Taking a deep breath, her lips curved into a thank-goodness-he's-not-proposing grin. She'd thought he actually might for a moment there. That would've been outrageous, a marriage proposal on a day like this. Even her brows lifted in relief. He'd grown so serious for a moment there that she'd honestly thought... She'd been afraid that he thought...

Oh. My. Hell. Ash Callahan wasn't smiling. *Oh, oh. He's really serious and... He's not talking about a simple stroll around the block, is he?*

"Ash?" she asked, her attention caught and her heart along with it. "W-walk with you?"

"Aye," he nodded, all five fingers now tucked in the back of her pants, where no one could see them strumming the swell of her ass. "I've nah got treasures to give you, nor gold at the end of your rainbow. If Quaid, Inc. is your calling, I'll follow, but Lass..." He drew in a deep breath, his eyes dark and not glancing away from her for even the space of a heartbeat. Her heartbeat. "Will you walk with me?" He said those five words with great deliberation.

Walk nothing. That wasn't what he meant at all. This walk *was* a marriage proposal. The Irish version. He didn't want a walk around the block, but around the moon. If Colby said yes, everything in her life would change. This would be a forever kind of a stroll through the rest of her life, with their hands held tight and their hearts clasped tighter. In sunshine and shadow. In storm and sunshine and...

Oh, for hell's sake! Now she was thinking as poetically as he talked.

But this was Ash Callahan. The prayerful poet. The dreamer.

The man who'd gone into her burning home to rescue her mom and her mom's dearest friend. The man who'd stabbed the two blood sucking vampires that had stalked Boston for too damned long. The man who, with every nick and gouge, every careful pare, cut and sweep of his wood carving tools while he'd perfected his masterpiece, the Irish pirate queen, Grace O'Malley, had also said a Hail Mary for Colby's safe return. For Colby, the woman who'd turned her back on him and left him behind, when she'd gone off to live her dream, never once considering that he would wait for her.

She swallowed hard, her heart suddenly stuck up so high in her sore throat. Did she dare accept his proposal? Should she open her heart and let this amazing, romantic, poetic man-who-put-stars-in-the-sky in?

"Yes," Colby breathed, her fingers suddenly at his ear, tugging him down to her mouth. "Yes, Ash. I'll walk with you tonight and tomorrow and every day for the rest of my life."

A tortured groan wound out of him as those hands of his slipped up and out of her pants to cup her head, his long fingers in her hair, his thumbs on her cheeks. Reverently, he drew her forward to his lips, brushing over hers before he lost all restraint and engulfed her mouth with a ragged growl. And there, in front of God and everyone else on the street, he kissed the hell out of her.

The thunder in his heart was her heartbeat, his breath in her face, her air. Colby knew it then. She could live forever on nothing but Ash.

CHAPTER TWENTY-NINE

The Cliffs of Mohr.

The Aran Islands.

Ashford Castle and only the best five-star bed-and-breakfasts in between. From Dublin to Shannon and from Belfast in the north to the southern shore of Dungarvin Bay, Ash O'Callaghan had returned to his homeland a hero instead of a pauper. His chin lifted the moment their Aer Lingus flight touched down to the Emerald Isle, forever the home of his heart. Not because he'd become a successful businessman in his absence, though, but because he'd become a lover and a husband, the ultimate protector of the fierce fighting woman at his side. He knew without a doubt that his mum and da would've been proud of Colby.

Very proud.

Remember that rich fellow from Cape Cod? He was none other than the sly Mitchell Rhoades himself. The crafty man had been taking care of the entire Quaid family behind-the-scenes for years. When he'd spied the dynamics, or at least, so he'd claimed, between Colby and Ash at one of her many soccer games, he'd done his homework like only Burton Quaid's devoted best friend could.

'Twas he who'd ordered the nautical figurehead from Ash, and 'twas he who'd put the spark of an idea in Ash's head to fashion it after the Irish pirate queen, 'if you'd please.' 'Twas also Mitchell Rhoades who'd ordered the lovely mermaid that commanded admiration from his office desk.

Aye, it was Ash's fault and his alone that the Irish pirate queen ended up looking like one of America's first female Rangers, but he blamed it on the magic in his fingers and the song in his heart at the time of the carving. 'Twas a good enough excuse even if he did come up with it himself.

It made Ash smile when Mitchell Rhoades needed a chair to set a spell on when at last he'd feasted his eyes on the original carved version of her royal self, Grace O'Malley. But it had also filled Ash's gut with an unexpected need to bash a chair over Rhoades' thick head for looking at Colby's naked carved body like he had.

Ash had curled his fingers to do the deed, when two words hissed out of Rhodes: "You're hired." Those words saved Mitch's life, is what they did. Abashed, Ash explained he wouldn't sell this version of Grace, that it held sentimental value beyond any amount of coinage, even those gold ones at the end of a Killarney rainbow. But Mitch was not an easy man to be dissuaded. With his hands on his knees, he'd pushed out of that chair, clapped Ash on the back as if they'd entered into a deal when Ash was fairly sure they hadn't.

Like the conniving gentleman he most certainly was, Mitch then extended the deadline to produce another figurehead, and, without blinking an eye, made Ash a job offer no man in his right mind could turn down, to come to work for Quaid, Inc., as special projects manager. Complete with an upfront signing bonus. A new warehouse, retooled and restocked with only the best modern equipment, the finest cedar and oak, pine and maple inventory North America could produce.

It seemed Mr. Mitchell Rhoades needed an expert carpenter in his alliance of professionals. He didn't seem to care that the one he wanted had recently experienced a devastating loss, as in that his entire warehouse and all of his tools had burnt to the bloody ground.

Ash accepted with grace, but on one condition. He wouldn't endanger the position Colby was currently learning, an apprenticeship with Mitch. A gentleman's handshake clinched the deal, and Ash found himself a successful businessman once again.

There he stood now, atop Rockfleet castle, the stone tower house of Grace O'Malley, with his body curled around the rarest feline in the world, the one and only, All American tigress of Boston, Mass. As lethal as she was, she was nah captured against her will, though. Aye, Colby fit in the cradle of his arms and chest, his hips and thighs, not as a prisoner, but willingly.

She not only fit, but she belonged, like a precious pearl to that lucky oyster in its shell, like the mythical fae of an Irish glen fit in the velvety petals of a rose. 'Twas the ultimate miracle of man and woman is what it was, the way Ash and Colby fit.

From the rooftop of Rockfleet Castle, they could see for miles. The city of Newport lay to the east, Mallaranny to the west. Beyond that the Atlantic, now tinged purple against a brilliant yellow-orange sunset. Beyond that, the end of Ash's rainbow, and—home.

"Tula called last night," Colby said, her chin lifted in defiance to the wind off the ocean. It tossed her hair in light gold streamers behind her.

"Aye, I heard you talking. Is everything okay?" he asked at her tiny ear, a curled shell so perfectly attuned to him that it sometimes seemed she read his mind before he'd so much as whispered what was on it.

"You'll never guess what the FBI found in Dugan's home." As in Hammer and Delores Dugan.

Please, do nah say wee bodies. Ash swallowed hard. After his last *visit* there, he wasn't sure he wanted to know what terrors lay inside their lovely, but unsettling, Cambridge residence. He'd wondered still what happened to their three children, though admittedly, he'd never once seen a school picture in all the years he'd known Hammer. Neither had Kevin.

"Dollzzzzzz," Colby whispered in a creepy, vibrato voice. "Delores and Hammer never had any children, but they had lots and lotszzzzz of dollzzzzzz." Again, with the creepy vibrato. "Everywhere. She'd had them sitting in chairs, on their sofa, and on shelves. Some were laid in beds and cradles with pacifiers and blankets. Teddy bears. Can you believe that? The FBI even found some dolls standing in corners as if they'd been punished." Colby shivered in his arms, snuggling her butt against his tired and very happy—but not dead—manhood. "Your friends were certifiable wack-jobs from *Psycho*, Ash. Where'd you meet them?"

Psycho? That must be another American movie he'd not yet seen. Wasn't going to now. "'Tis no wonder there was no sign of life at their house when I went looking for him. If you must know, Kevin and I met Hammer at the pub one night, but I'd nah met Delores until that day." He'd rather talk about Bella. "How's Mum?"

Colby ducked her neck into her shoulders. "She's happy to be home. Thank you for installing that elevator. It's made things easier for Tula, too. And thanks for cleaning the wooden panels and the eagle in her entryway. I think seeing her home being restored has given Mom a new burst of life.

Tula said she started playing bridge with her girlfriends yesterday. She tossed that ridiculous turban out, too. And did you see how pretty her hair was styled at our wedding?"

"Aye, I did. She's got girlfriends?" Imagining *girls* that age was a stretch.

But it was true. Bella'd had a good coat of glossy red lipstick on her mouth at the wedding, and her hair was dyed. Ash had it straight from Mitch that her doctor had changed her meds. Bella didn't have Alzheimer's, but she was dehydrated, the underlying cause of her dizzy spells and memory loss. Mitch saw to it that a live-in nurse joined forces with Tula in keeping up with the matron of the mighty Quaid empire.

"I laughed when she called them old biddies." Colby's chuckle resonated all the way to his groin. "I mean, look at her, Ash. Mom's no spring chicken. She's probably older than most all of her friends."

He nuzzled his nose into the tangled curls of Colby's hair, diving for the warm crook of her neck. She was the one who put stars in the sky now. Her unconditional love of him worked magic on his male ego, too. His swagger was back, and his zest for life as well.

Colby's arm curled over his head, holding him to her. Ah, the scent of roses, wind, and gunpowder. 'Twas nothing like it in the world, nor ever would be.

In all his wildest fantasies, Ash had never savored a woman so deeply, nor loved one as fiercely. With her tucked against him, he could see down her knit top, straight to the delicious valley between the plump breasts he intended to suckle at the first possible chance.

One crook of her little finger and he was a man not only brought to attention—mighty stiff attention at that—but brought to his knees at the sublime mercy of his new pirate queen. Smitten was he. Plundered, whipped, and bewitched.

"You owe me a walk, Wife," he murmured, his voice gone hoarse at the power of this tiny thing.

Colby twisted in his arms, her lovely breasts molded to his chest and his blood turning to lava again. "I owe you my life, Husband," she whispered, her lips drawn into a pout that signaled she meant to kiss him.

Ash pressed a warm, wet kiss to her mouth, and a little bit of tongue as well. Standing there with his future spread before him and his heart on fire, he was never more certain...

His All-American girl had stolen his Irish heart away.

CHAPTER THIRTY

Colby stood at a quaint little cemetery in Mayo County Ireland. One broad headstone faced her. Thomas and Annie O'Callaghan's. Ash had already taken his place, sitting cross-legged before his parents, his hands on his knees as if he were simply home and wanted to chat. Peering up at Colby, he patted the clover at his side. "Come sit with me, love. I want you to meet me folks."

That was awkward, Ash speaking as if the dead could hear him. Dropping to her knees, Colby joined him, at a loss for words. "It's so green here," was all she could come up with.

"Aye, you're in Ireland." He wrapped an arm around her. "'Tis green everywhere."

That it was. Jackdaws chattered from the boughs of a nearby tree, so large and wide it could've easily been several hundred years old. To the side of the cemetery, an ivy-covered stone church promised salvation from the moss stained cross mounted at its spire. Colby wasn't a churchgoer, not like Ash. She'd seen too much of the world to trust the philosophies of man mingled with holy words and supposed divine promises.

"Mum. Da," Ash said with a deep sigh. "This is Colby Quaid Callahan, me wife. I've taken her to me heart, and I want you to love her as much as I do."

Colby stared at the marker, still not feeling the same mystical connection with his parents that he did. The black marble headstone was thoughtfully done, a tribute to Ash's love for them. The carved family name, O'Callaghan, graced the moss-covered, foot-high base in bold gold lettering. Thomas's name was etched in the center of the left panel, Annie's on the right. Beneath those names were dates of births and deaths. Some Gaelic words Colby didn't understand.

She cleared her throat, needing to be there for Ash, but uncomfortable in what was definitely a graveyard, not a lovely cottage. "This is nice," she offered lamely.

He nodded, wordless, an unusual feat for a charmer of his magnitude. 'Twas then Colby looked at him with her heart and saw that his eyes brimmed with unshed tears. Her big-talking Irishman was biting his lower lip. Trying to be tough.

Circling an arm around his waist, she told him in case he didn't know, "I'm sorry, Ash. I can't imagine what losing them did to you."

Another head nod and a stiff, "Aye." He growled to clear his throat. "I came home from college early that day, but the deed was already done. The house was burnt, the constable and firemen were on the scene. I was... too late."

She could tell this gnawed at him. "There wasn't anything you could've done. You didn't kill them."

"Aye, 'twas Liam who did that." Another deep sigh. Another long minute before Ash said, "He came home early that morning as well, hiding from the law after he'd bombed the constabulary in Belfast. Three men were killed in that blast, and the authorities were hunting for him and his bloody friends. But Da would nah let Liam in and so they fought." Ash shook his head, not so much in anger as—lost. "He knocked me da to the ground, then dragged him inside with her. Said if he was nah welcome, no one would be again. Then he started the fire. Diesel burns hot and fast. 'Twas still smoking when I got home. Everyone in Newport could see it."

Colby cringed at the horror of losing his parents that way. "They were alive?" This part she hadn't known.

"Aye." A tremor shuddered up his spine. "They were when he... when he..."

"Oh, Ash, baby, I'm so sorry." Colby pressed her face to his bicep, holding him close. "What a bastard your brother is. Now I'm glad I knifed him. I should've killed him." *I should've asked exactly what happened to your parents a long time ago instead of finding out now. Why didn't I?*

"'Twas always him or me," Ash murmured, his voice gone soft and sad. "One of us has to die."

"Then it'll be him," she declared fervently. Somehow. Someway. "Did he tell you this? Is that how you know what happened?"

A small grunt. "The bloody braggart made sure I knew every last detail. How long before the fire brigade showed. How much they screamed until..." Ash scrubbed a hand over his face, trembling at the ungodly memory. "He said he'd do the same to me the next time he saw me, so do nah feel one bit of guilt for taking him on. He would've killed you if you had nah." Ash had slipped into his Irish brogue, a sure sign of the depth of his pain.

"Please tell me what that means?" she pleaded, pointing to the Gaelic etched below Thomas's name, needing Ash to not dwell on things he couldn't change.

"*Suaimhneas,*" Ash said easily. "'Tis Gaelic for peace and comfort. Da deserved a hundredfold of peace and rest after the hard life he lived. For working the fields and keeping his Catholic faith despite the lures of the world. For being the wisest man I ever knew." He wiped his misty eyes. "Ah, he could make me laugh. Mum, too. You would've loved him, and he you, Lass. He came from a long line of Thomases, his father and his father's father before him. All Thomas O'Callaghans. Until me and... until Liam."

Colby calmed, understanding now why Ash had needed to visit his parents. It wasn't closure he was seeking, but some small measure of that same comfort he'd given his father.

Ash pointed to Annie's side of the stone and the Gaelic words etched there. "That describes me Mum through and through. 'Twas never a day went by she did nah bake a loaf for a neighbor or tend a sick child. She loved children most of all."

"She loved you," Colby breathed. She didn't believe in Irish magic or superstitions, but there was definitely something in the air between this broad headstone and Ash. It raised the hairs up the back of her neck, almost as if the two beings he loved the most were here with him.

"Aye, I know that now." Ash swiped a hand over his face. "And I loved her. More than I ever told her."

Colby didn't dare try to pronounce the Irish words. Any way she tried, the phrase ended up with a Spanish twist. *Bean an tí.* "Say it for me, Ash." *Let me hear the love you have for your mother.*

He let out a deep sigh, his shoulders relaxed as he pronounced, "Ban-a-tee. It means *'she who cares for everything'.* Even me."

Colby could've cried. *I was wrong about Mom and Dad. About Quaid, Inc., and Mitchell Rhoades. And now I'm wrong about this, too. Unbelievable.*

He'd been raised by devout Catholic parents, who'd worked the land for generations. That was where he'd gotten his sexist ideas, simply because that was the way it was. Annie and Thomas weren't rich, but it was obvious they'd loved their sons. Seeing this side of his mother, the one who'd watched over him since he was a baby, the one who'd cradled him and taught him all those prayers he'd said while carving his pirate queen. The one who'd washed his dirty face and kissed his scrapes and little-boy bruises...

It seemed that Annie O'Callaghan, *she who cares for everything,* was still taking care of Ash—through Colby. Still teaching in her humble Irish way. Colby knew now that her parents had always loved her, *in their way.* She also knew Ash would die defending her. That he'd fight fiercely to protect her if she needed it or not. That he loved her. *In his way.*

What's more, there was honor in taking care of your man at the end of a hard day, and she wanted nothing more than to be like Annie in that respect and lighten his load. She'd fought so hard to be a separate entity, to be strong enough to stand alone, only to understand now there was no shame in being an equal partner—a soul mate— with this man. If he'd let her.

"You owe me a walk, Husband," she reminded

him, tears welling.

Ash pulled her to her feet but kept hold of her fingers. "Aye," he said quietly, his gaze warm and tender, "and I owe you this." Tugging her right hand to his lips, he kissed her knuckles while at the same time, he slipped a gold ring onto her index finger. "This was Mum's," he said, the blue of his eyes swallowed up with the black. "It's all I have left of her, Lass, and she would want you to have it."

Colby could hardly catch her breath, her heart pinched so hard. The ring was a simple gold band, embossed with two twining roses, a vine connecting them. Though the ring was tarnished, the gold petals of the roses gleamed.

She decided to tell him right then and there. "You're wrong, Ash. This isn't all you have of your mother. Thomas and Annie are still here. I can feel them. Can't you?"

Trembling, because never in a million years had she seen this for herself, Colby brought his big, warm hand to her belly. They'd been married three months now, two of those months spent touring Ireland. But the wee one growing in her womb was a kicking four-month old fetus, ready to put his—or her—stars in the skies.

Ash cocked his head. "Since when?" he asked,

his tone raspy and unbelieving.

"Since the first night in your apartment," Colby confessed. "I wasn't sure until yesterday."

"You were pregnant when we wed?" Ah, she adored the wicked gleam in his beautiful eyes. "That's why you needed to get to a drugstore yesterday. You bought a pregnancy test, did you nah?"

"Aye," she said coyly. "And some chocolate." Cherry-chocolates to be exact. *Food cravings. Who knew?*

With a cry, the crazy man she loved with every beat of her heart dropped to his knees in the grass. Easing one warm hand under her shirt, he palmed her bare belly, then lifted her shirt and pressed a warm, fervent kiss to her skin. "'Tis a wee boy, I can tell by his fine heartbeat."

"She's a girl," Colby countered, threading her fingers over Ash's scalp and through the thick waves he'd let grow. "A fine strapping girl who'll be able to take care of herself."

Ash was already shaking his head before Colby finished. "Nah! Trust me on this, Lass. A man knows when his woman's about to give him a son."

"A daughter!" Colby declared, laughter

bubbling up from her heart at this capricious man she loved so hard.

"A boy," his stubborn self insisted.

"A girl! And her name is Annie!"

That shut Ash up. he looked up at her then, the sun on his forehead and a universe of stars shining in his sparkling blue eyes. "Aye, you might be right. That'd be just like me mum to send you a partner in crime before she sent me a son. Annie 'tis."

Did you know pregnant women tend to get emotional as quick as lightning, more so when they win a silly argument over the gender of their first love child? Tears brimmed at the adoration Colby saw on this Irishman's handsome face. "Boy or girl," she told him honestly, her voice gone tight and squeaky. "It's all the same to me. Your mum and da will love *her* from heaven just as much as—"

"—we'll love *him* from here." Ash climbed to his feet but kept his palm on Colby's belly as he threw back his head and yelled, "I'm soon to be a father! A good father! Just like me da! Do you hear me, Liam? You chose badly. You lose!"

Colby choked back a sob, so proud of her husband. She could almost feel Thomas and Annie smiling down from heaven on their son.

On her, too. Wiping her tears—*damn those hormones!*—she whispered, "Take me back to our room, Husband. I need to make love to you for the rest of the day."

With his arm already around her neck, he tugged her forehead to his lips. "Aye," he muttered, placing a warm, wet kiss on her nose. "And all the night long, too."

It was Colby's turn to sigh. She'd finally found what she hadn't known she'd been looking for. Contentment. Peace. He hadn't found it in Boston, Texas, nor in far off Cambodia. It wasn't in some fancy house overlooking the Pacific Coast of California, either. It was here. Inside the circle of Ash's arms. Like the words of her marriage vow, wherever Ash went, she would be at his side. For richer or for poorer. In sickness and in health. For better or for worse.

Like an Army Ranger. Leading the way. *Most of the time.*

The End

Thank you for reading Ash's story!

Be sure to check out the guys and gals from The TEAM in Irish Winters' series: *In the Company of Snipers*

Other Irish Winters' books:

King of Hearts, Deuces Wild Series, #1
Joker Joker, Deuces Wild Series, #2
One-Eyed Jack, Deuces Wild Series, #3
Smoke, Hearts and Ashes Series, #1
Angel, An SOBs Novel, #1

Coming soon

Assassin, An SOBs Novel, #2
Ace, Deuces Wild Series, #4

YOU ARE THE KEY TO THIS BOOK'S SUCCESS!

Please tell other readers why you like Ash and Colby's story by leaving an honest review at the retail site where you purchased it.

Recommend it to your friends. Lend it.

Most of all, enjoy it!

The best way to keep up with my new releases, giveaways, and actionable intel is to sign up for my spam-free newsletter at IrishWinters.com.

About the Author

Irish Winters

...is a best-selling author who, when she isn't writing, dabbles in poetry, grandchildren, and rarely—as in extremely rarely—the kitchen. More prone to be outdoors than in, she grew up the quintessential tomboy on a dairy farm in rural Wisconsin, spent her teenage years in the Pacific

Northwest, but calls the Wasatch Mountains of Northern Utah, home. For now. She believes in making every day count for something, and follows the wise admonition of her mother to, "Look out the window and see something!"

Connect with Irish online:

On Facebook
https://www.facebook.com/author.irishwinters

On Twitter: https://twitter.com/irishwinters1

Or visit www. IrishWinters.com

www.ingramcontent.com/pod-product-compliance
Lightning Source LLC
Chambersburg PA
CBHW050816190726
48286CB00007B/1890